The Trouble with Playing Cupid

by

Tamara Philip

Vanilla Heart Publishing

The Trouble with Playing Cupid
by Tamara Philip

Published by: Vanilla Heart Publishing
www.VanillaHeartBookAndAuthors.com
10121 Evergreen Way, 25-156
Everett, WA 98204 USA

ISBN-13: 978-0692286470 ISBN-10: 0692286470

10 9 8 7 6 5 4 3 2 1 First Edition

First Printing, September 2014
Printed in the United States of America

The Trouble with Playing Cupid

by

Tamara Philip

Table of Contents

Dedication and Acknowledgements

Bonus Preview
Diary of a Big Dummy

Book Club Discussion Starters

Tamara Philip Author Bio and Photo

Dedication

To my Mom and Dad,
who believed in me even when I didn't deserve it.

Acknowledgements

Natalie Gilbert, I am eternally grateful for your insane yellow highlighter skills, sheer dedication to making sure my manuscript was worth submitting and our enduring friendship.

Jane Vaughan, for being the best future mother in law a girl could ever ask for.

To my sisters for rereading this book 50 million times each and never complaining, I love you guys!

My niece Meilani, thank you for being wonderful and keeping me on my toes.

An extra special Thank you to my FF.net girlfriends who I was lucky enough to get to know and adore. Especially you, Amee Parmenter.

and Chris Vaughan for being my champion and the love of my life.

Chapter One

"I can't believe I let Trace talk me into singing on his show on such short notice. Doesn't he know I have to perform at the Critics' Awards tomorrow in LA? And not just once but twice! I'm going to be exhausted. That's like an eight hour flight from Vancouver!" December whined as her stylist fussed over her rapidly wilting curls.

Terrence smiled sympathetically at her reflection in the mirror but kept quiet otherwise. He knew how she got when she was ranting. God help him if he tried to soothe her. It would only lead to her being snippy with him, and he really didn't need the hassle today.

December Brown was a contrary sort of person. A successful singer in her prime, she was charming, warm, and generous to a fault. She was also a tireless defender of the downtrodden. Acutely aware of social issues, she supported as many charities and foundations as humanly possible. According to the media, she was a regular bleeding heart. Yet in her personal life, the incredibly private twenty-eight year old was more of a couch potato, choosing to spend evenings on the internet for hours at a time rather than go to the countless parties and non-fundraising events she was invited to. She was one of life's 'refusers'. She wasn't a quitter, since she usually couldn't even be bothered to try. If it seemed like a competition in any shape or form, she would opt out long before she knew the odds. There was only one reason she was in the limelight now, and it wasn't a secret ambitious drive. It was because her PR agent, who was also her best friend since adolescence, insisted on it.

If Clarissa Gregory hadn't pulled her up by her bootstraps and forced her to utilize her talents, Terrence feared December would still be trying to save the world, one homeless shelter at a time. Probably while wearing bright orange sweatpants and the rattiest pair of ballet flats he'd ever laid eyes on, just like she wore the day they'd met and he saved her by befriending the biggest fashion misfit that walked the earth. He later found out she'd traded her sneakers for the holey replacements with a teenager whose family resided in the shelter. The fourteen year old was skipping school to avoid the bullying her predicament brought to her. Back then, December couldn't afford to buy new shoes for the girl, so she gave the pair on her feet. Nowadays, she generously donated both time and money to Backpack America and various other charities to ensure no other child suffered like that girl did.

Sadly however, the orange sweatpants were all December.

"Eight hours on the plane, then maybe three hours of sleep, only to start rehearsing for like four more hours until my actual performance...Oh God I'm going to miss my soap operas," she lamented, looking more and more irate.

"Girl, hush! You're ruining your make-up with all that frowning." Terrence interrupted, retouching her glossy petal pink lipstick. "Now the reason you're on this show is because Trace is your friend and you adore him. Remember?" He looked at December's still frowning face expectantly. She nodded reluctantly, but her mouth remained firmly closed. Still, she pinched him for good measure.

"...and Clarissa would murder you if you didn't perform tonight." Terrence continued even as she sighed in exasperation. "This is good publicity, Dee! 'Trace Randall Tonight' is the most watched talk show in North America. Anybody who is anybody wants on here, and you were invited."

December rolled her eyes in acceptance. She knew Terrence was right. Especially about her murder at the hands of Clarissa, her best friend slash publicist slash manager slash evil overlord.

"Fine, Okay. But I want IHOP after this. And don't look at me like that, Terry. I'm getting my pancakes, thighs be damned!" She stood up and adjusted her leather mini skirt, with as much attitude as one could muster while doing such a thing. Terrence sucked his teeth, and smoothed down the iridescent pearl colored sequins of her tank top.

"Deal! Now go sing the hell out of that song."

"Wait, who are the other guests on tonight? I forgot to ask earlier." December asked as she teetered on six inch stiletto heels towards the stagehand that was waiting patiently for her.

She received no reply from Terrence, who'd disappeared into the back of the dressing room with a pile of clothes for wardrobe. The stagehand didn't seem very forthcoming either as he pushed her towards the Green Room to await her cue. December shrugged, swallowing down the butterflies in her tummy that never failed to show up when she had to sing in front of a live audience.

"Alright folks, you're in for a treat tonight. The ever glorious songstress, December Brown, will be performing her latest chart topper," Trace Randall announced, smiling proudly as the crowd went wild. "...and that's not all, she'll be joining us on stage here for a special chat after!"

Once the applause died down, he continued on with his announcement "But first, let's welcome all the way from Hollywood by way of Great Britain, the insanely handsome, Tom Elmswood."

In his expertly tailored steel gray suit, Tom smiled and waved as he walked over to Trace, hugging him tightly before they both sat down on the big dark blue couch.

"Tom, it's great to see you. I'm so glad you could make time for us what with being named 'The Sexiest Man in the World' and all." Trace laughed as the ladies in the crowd screamed their appreciation.

Tom grinned sheepishly. He ran his hand through his neatly cut, short black hair nervously. "Thanks for having me, Trace. I don't know about the sexy stuff but...thank you all for the support."

"Isn't he dreamy, ladies? Look at how pink his ears are!" Trace teased mercilessly. "Anyway, Tom, you've been busy this year with all those movies and interviews and everything, right? I bet you're sick to death of having to talk about that stuff?"

Tom eyed Trace warily. Everyone knew that Trace Randall never asked the normal questions. Since the show was only a half hour long, he always aimed for the most personal and uncomfortable stuff, which left his guests reeling, but his fans talking. Tom inwardly groaned, knowing how much he didn't want to do this show, but his manager had insisted, citing that he needed as much publicity as he could get.

"No, I love talking about the movies I'm so lucky to be a part of. I don't think I could ever get sick of being able to entertain people." He responded, earnestly.

"Aw, that's sweet! But I don't care about the movies right now. Neither does my audience, right people?" Trace nodded to the sound of audience approval. "So let's talk about Tom Elmswood. You lead a pretty private life, don't you? I mean, we barely see you in any of the magazines or tabloids. Tell us about you."

Tom licked his suddenly dry lips. "Well, um, I'm a little too old to be out partying all the time, so I like to stay close to home when I don't have to work."

"Old? Tom, you're only thirty four! If you want to talk about old, I'm nearly forty five and I look sixty five." Trace quipped genially, putting Tom at ease.

"So tell us, where's home these days?"

"Well I'm originally from Northampton, England and I have a small country house there where I spend each summer. But while in America, I have a condo in Manhattan. It's not home yet but it serves its purpose."

"So, let's see... you're a homebody and you lead a quiet existence. Okay, now it's time to get to the juicy stuff. Is there a special lady in your life?" Trace leaned closer, his deep brown eyes twinkling mischievously.

"Uh, no...not at the moment..." Tom gulped. The look of triumph Trace gave him did not bode well.

"How sad..." Trace looked anything but. In fact, his blindingly white grin spread to epic proportions. "Tell me, why aren't you dating any of your glamorous co-stars?"

"Oh they're entirely too lovely to be stuck home with the likes of me." Tom admitted truthfully. The audience swooned at his words.

"Ladies, did you hear him? Could we vote for him all over again please? Tom Elmswood, folks! Let's give him a round of applause!" Trace implored, clapping enthusiastically himself. "When we come back from the break, December Brown will be singing for us!"

December lost herself in her music as she sang and danced to the beat her band played. She always put her all in each of her performances and 'Trace Randall Tonight' was no different. The audience gave her a standing ovation as she blew them kisses and walked backstage at the end of her set.

She was sweaty and probably looked shiny and gross. All she wanted to do was find Terrence and go get her blueberry pancakes.

"Change of plans, Dee. Trace is doing a short interview with you first. Don't argue, Clarissa agreed to it. So stand still so I can fix you up," Terrence demanded as he blotted her face roughly. He kept his gaze averted. He knew if he made eye contact with December after telling her that news, she would go ballistic. He continued talking rapidly, intentionally ignoring her attempts to interrupt him. "Clarissa said she'll have a big hot pile of blueberry pancakes waiting in your hotel room, if you do it. She'll explain later."

December huffed and puffed but there was no house to blow down so she quietly fumed. She fumed while Terrence applied fresh deodorant spray to her underarms, and she raged as another stagehand directed her towards where Trace stood with his arms outstretched, waiting for her to walk into them.

All her anger melted away once Trace folded her into a warm embrace. When his large, muscular body blocked out the view of the stage, and muffled the loud sound of applause, December remembered she liked Trace. She liked the way he always twirled her dark copper locks as if it was spun gold whenever he came over for coffee, and that with his bright red hair and big brown eyes, he never failed to look excited about life. When she'd met Trace four years ago, at an awards show after-party, they became instant friends. So many text messages and lunch dates later, December could forgive Trace just about anything.

"December Brown, you never fail to look magnificent." Trace said as he pulled away to grin at her, before kissing her sweetly on each side of her face.

"Thank you for having me, Trace. I missed you." December suddenly felt misty-eyed and a little foolish. How could she have been so grumpy about this interview when it was Trace doing it?

"Did you hear her, people? She missed little ol' me!" Trace beamed happily, as he ushered her over to sit down.

"Have a seat next to Tom, sweetheart."

December turned to say hello to her co-guest. She stopped in her tracks when she saw Tom Elmswood sitting there, smiling gorgeously at her. Her heart flip-flopped heavily in her chest. She was going to kill Clarissa. And probably Trace. It was going to be on the 10 o'clock news.

December must have looked alarmed, because she watched Tom's smile falter at the sight of her face, but then it was replaced with a sympathetic one. Ugh, now he thought she was pathetic. And so very sweaty. Oh God, it was high school all over again.

December felt hot and itchy with nerves, but hauled her game face on. You smile and greet. That's what you do when you meet a new person. Even if that person was your secret celebrity crush. Well, 'crush' really wasn't the word. It was too light and friendly. Tom Elmswood was her secret celebrity boyfriend. And on some days her secret fiancé. Clarissa knew. And Terrence knew. Oh God, now she had to kill Terrence too. Did they have the death sentence in New York State? Never mind. It would be worth it.

Hopefully Trace didn't know. That's what fortified December's resolve. She straightened her smile out until she thought it looked friendly, and walked over to where Tom sat. Where she was supposed to sit - next to him. Her scalp tingled with warmth at the thought. Tom stood up and took her hand, pulling her into a half hug.

"It's so lovely to meet you, Miss Brown." He whispered, followed by a gently placed kiss on her cheek. December whimpered in reply. He smelled amazing.

Tom smiled and helped her to her seat. He sat so close she could practically run her hands through his impeccably cut raven locks. She nearly had to sit on her hands to keep from doing just that.

"December, we're so glad that you could join us. Folks, this woman is something special, isn't she? What a fantastic voice!" Trace blathered on but December's mind was still on the fact that Tom's lips touched her cheek. "So December, I have the pleasure of being one of your closest friends, don't I?"

"Err. What? Yes, duh. I adore you." She quickly remembered where she was and tried to be as normal as possible.

"See guys, I wasn't lying. She does know me." Trace joked while his audience laughed. "So I don't need to ask her all about her life, since I pretty much know it all. P.S., she's as bad as Tom. Obviously she loves her privacy too, since she, like Tom, is never in a magazine unless it's a photo shoot or interview. Did you know that, Tom? Are you a fan of hers?"

Tom looked embarrassed, but said diplomatically, "This was the first time that I've heard her sing but I'm already a fan."

"Tom lives under a rock, people. You heard it here first." Trace said looking merrily shocked.

"I don't really listen to the radio." Tom admitted, bashfully.

Trace shook his head in mock disgust. "Well you need to grab her CDs. This is her third album, after all!"

"Trace, stop bullying him! You don't have to listen, Mr. Elmswood," December spoke up, giving Trace an icy glare.

21

"But I want to. And I will. And, call me Tom," he said, touching her hand to get her attention. December whipped around to face him, looking equal parts delighted and mortified. His stormy blue eyes sparkled back at her.

"Oh, um, sorry, I'm December..." she stuttered, her light brown skin flushing rosily. Tom held her gaze, as she melted into a puddle on the inside.

"Oh my God, aren't they so cute?" Trace placed his hand over his heart and feigned swooning, while the audience cooed. December smelled a rat but she couldn't quite put her finger on it.

"Please tell me you've seen her in the latest Sports Illustrated Swimsuit Edition or Marie Claire at least?"

With each magazine name, the photo spread in question flashed up on the large screen behind Trace's head so Tom could see. He looked suitably impressed at the images of December in a blood red evening gown and Gothic make-up, and several shots of her, in a shiny silver bikini, frolicking on the beach. December shot daggers at Trace. Why was he pushing this? Obviously Tom hadn't known who she was until tonight.

"You look particularly fetching in that bathing suit, December." She blushed prettily at Trace's compliment.

"Honestly like seventy eight percent of that is Photoshop. My trainer wishes with all his heart that I looked that good," December admitted, laughing. She remembered she had an impressionable fan base that had to know that they didn't need to strive for falsely advertised perfection.

"Nonsense, you look gorgeous tonight. You can't give Photoshop credit for that." Trace was laying it on thick, she noted.

"True. Terrence Mitchell, my stylist and makeup artist, is a genius. He deserves a raise... but don't tell him that," she said conspiratorially, earning a round of laughter and applause.

"She's so humble. Tom, do you see how lovely she is?" Trace prodded with not even an ounce of subtlety.

December fought the urge to kick him in the shin. Why was he being so shameless?

"Don't answer that, Tom. Trace is just trying to get uninvited to my birthday party this year." She said lightly, attempting to change the subject.

"Now, December darling, I know you're getting a little irritated at me already. But you'll forgive me in time. I hope...yikes," Trace pleaded, dramatically.

"Of course I forgive you, Trace. Wait. What do you mean 'in time'?" December tore her gaze from Tom to glower at Trace.

"Well, remember New Year's Eve when you sent me that drunken text?"

"No, I do not. And you should probably delete that," December said, warningly. Her eyes did an odd pleading, threatening hybrid glare to which Trace shook his head, uncompromisingly.

"No can do, kiddo. This is for your own good. It's time Uncle Trace played Matchmaker."

Chapter Two

Oh God, No! So, Trace did know about her crush on Tom. December wished with all her might to disappear. Or at least for Trace to turn into a pebble. Neither happened.

"Since you don't remember that text message, I'll have to remind you. Who wants to see December's drunken text?" Trace asked grandly, to an already foaming at the mouth crowd. "Don't you want to see it too, Tom?"

"Not if she doesn't want us to, Trace." Tom said, kindly and December fell in love all over again. She might as well enjoy the feeling while it lasted because once Tom saw it, things would become very awkward. She hid her face in her hands and squeezed her eyes really tight, hoping for a power shortage.

"Trust me, Tom. You need to see this. Sorry, Dee. Remember I love you and only want you to get out of your shell." Trace said the last part quietly but December resigned herself to the fall out. "Here we go, people!"

She knew by the hoots and hollers from the crowd that they saw her message. She refused to open her eyes; instead she decided some things. No more drinking. And no more text messaging. Okay wait she couldn't stop text messaging. Never mind, just no more sending texts while drinking. And none to Trace, ever again. She could live with that.

Suddenly she felt soft lips on the shell of her ear, and a lightly accented voice whispering into it.

"You can look now, December. The worst is over." She stiffened at his touch. God, why did Tom have to smell so freaking good? And why did Trace have to be so evil? Oh well. Time to face the music.

December slowly sat up and opened her eyes. Ignoring Trace and Tom, she stared directly at the words on the screen:

"OMG TRACE, DID YOU SEE TOM ELMSWOOD'S NEW MOVIE YET? GOD, HE'S SO HOT. WHY CAN'T HE BE MY BOYFRIEND?? SHOULD I SEND HIM TOPLESS PICTURES?? OMG DELETE THIS. WHY AREN'T YOU REPLYING? OH YEA, THIS IS A TEXT. BUT SERIOUSLY MY NEW YEAR'S RESOLUTION IS TO MAKE OUT WITH TOM ELMSWOOD. MAYBE GET TO THIRD BASE. YAY! SHH DON'T TELL NOBODY LOLOL."

Ugh, it was even worse than she thought. December wanted to vomit. Preferably on Trace. She tore her eyes away from those horribly humiliating words and drew on previously untapped inner strength to keep it together because she was still on live television. She put on a fake smile and pretended to think it was funny.

"Trace, you are so dead to me!" She chuckled but meant every word.

Trace reached out to grab her hand but she pulled back into her seat, folding her hands neatly onto her lap. December acted in tons of her music videos. She could act like she wasn't about to die of shame for at least another two minutes.

She leaned in closer to Tom and whispered, "I am so sorry about this. I didn't know."

"Don't worry about it." He whispered back, squeezing her hand in support.

Oh, but she did worry. She knew he would never speak to her again. Then again, he didn't know who she was before tonight. So, hooray, at least she'd get to go back to loving him from afar. Minus a few friends.

"So, Tom... what do you think of December's proclamation?" Trace questioned just as enthusiastically as before, as if he hadn't just thrown her to the wolves.

As soon as the show was over, she was going to delete his number. Trace would be blocked and banned so hard it would make his stupid big head spin. She would keep Terrence, though. He was probably an innocent bystander in all of this.

December felt Tom's hand resting lightly on her back, trying and failing to provide silent solidarity. She chanced a glance at him.

"Well, she's extremely beautiful...," he said slowly, drawing the words out. He left the sentence as is, open ended. The crowd ate it up. It was suggestive enough for them to be happy and ambiguous enough that he hadn't actually answered the question. December didn't know if she wanted to cry or laugh. She chose a mixture of both, a choked kind of laugh that was lost in the audience's elation.

"You heard it first here, people! A love match in the making! Thank you to December and Tom for joining us. That's all, folks! Have a great night!" Trace announced at the ending of the program.

December sat rigid for the requisite two minutes to allow the credits to roll and the cameras to pan out, her face a picture of pleasantness as she smiled emptily. However the second the cameras started shutting down, she was off like a shot. She ignored Trace's yells for her to come back, and headed for her dressing room. She needed a good cry.

Terrence Mitchell knew how this would turn out from the second Clarissa explained to him what Trace wanted to do; therefore, he had the tissues prepared. It was a cruel stunt to play on someone you considered a friend, even if it was for her own good. They all worried for December. She was so afraid of getting hurt that she rarely took a risk where her heart was concerned. She lived in her dream bubble, with her fantasy boyfriend, Tom. In reality, she hardly ever dated. The closest to dating was in her music videos when she had to pretend a random model was the man of her dreams. And when said models tried to actually ask her out, she'd run for the hills. Burying herself in web surfing and as much fan fiction a person could read in twenty four hours.

At 5'5", with sparkling hazel eyes, and a flawless cafe au lait complexion complimented by chestnut colored hair that fell below her shoulders, she was beautiful. And yet, instead of flaunting her enviably hot stuff, she shied away from romantic situations because there was a very big chance her heart might be broken. Unsurprisingly, she was extremely afraid of being abandoned, given her shady origins.

For a person in her profession, which dealt in luck and not always in talent, she was, surprisingly, a pessimistic risk avoider. Especially when it came to dating. In fact, Terrence could count on one hand how many quasi-serious relationships December had with the opposite sex since they'd met six years earlier. Unfortunately for her, he wasn't the only one who'd noticed her lack of boyfriends. Anyone else would have started slowly by introducing her to single friends at conveniently held dinner parties, but not Trace. He just had to play cupid in front of a live TV audience.

December burst through the dressing room door, flinging herself into his arms, sobbing her guts out like he knew she would.

"Why would he do this to me, Terr? What kind of butthead move was that?" She asked, despairingly.

"He thought he was fulfilling your fantasy, sweetie. In Trace's crazy mind, he felt like he was doing you a favor," Terrence explained.

"Well, he's a jerk. And now I look like a loser in Tom's eyes forever. He didn't even know who I was..." Tears streamed down her pretty face. He sighed, thank God for waterproof mascara or else she'd look a horrible sight.

"It's his loss, because you are fabulous." He hugged her tight and kissed her forehead. "Let's get you home."

"Yes, let's go before someone tries to come console me or question me some more." She perked up, yanking her coat on and pulling a hat roughly on her head.

"Do you want to go see Tom?" Terrence asked cautiously.

"What? No. Why?" Her eyebrows furrowed in a genuine terror at the very idea.

"To apologize about the text. And for Trace putting him on the spot like that. He wasn't expecting it either. It's going to be his name all over the tabloids tomorrow along with yours."

"But I already apologized on stage!" Terrence shot her a judging look. "Okay, fine. I'll go now before he leaves the studio, just to get it over with. I'll meet you back here in five minutes, okay? How do I look?" December asked as she wiped her eyes with the back of her hand, while yanking off her hat.

"Do you really want me to answer that?" Terrence said sassily

"Oh shush. I'll put my hair into a pony tail. Will that help?"

"Greatly. And blow your nose. You sound like hell."

"Yes, Mom." She giggled into her tissue.

December quickly stepped into the hallway that led to Tom's dressing room. She stopped to fix her clothes before knocking, but voices stilled her actions.

"It was awful. How embarrassing was that? I could strangle Trace myself."

"It wasn't that bad, she's very successful. As crushes go, she's a gift from the gods."

"I don't care about that. Now everyone will expect us to go out on a date. Or flirt or something awful like that."

December cringed. Dating her would be awful for him? He sounded so disgusted at the idea of having to flirt with her. She wanted to go home and curl up in her big fluffy bed and not see anyone for at least forty-eight hours. Her stomach hurt. Her heart hurt. Hot tears burned at her already red rimmed eyes and she could barely breathe. She stumbled away to find Terrence. December couldn't handle any more heartache or humiliation. She wanted to go home and forget about all this night but she had the Critics' Awards the next day. After that, though, she wasn't leaving the house for a week. And anyone who tried to stop her was going to get knifed.

The ride in the rented limo back to the hotel was filled with December's quiet sobs.

"What happened, sweetness? You can tell me. It can't be that bad." Terrence rubbed her back in light circles as she curled into herself.

"The very idea of being with me makes him sick to his stomach!" She began crying even louder.

Terrence sat holding her in stunned surprise. Well, that kind of thing would make anyone bawl their eyes out. He whispered soothing words into her hair, and only vaguely registered that this wasn't their normal West Coast driver.

When they arrived at the hotel penthouse, a large stack of blueberry pancakes for December and scrambled eggs with toast for Terrence awaited them. December took off her shoes and stomped towards her bedroom, stating she wasn't hungry.

"We have to leave at four in the morning to be there in time at the airport. But until then, if anyone calls, tell them I'll talk to them tomorrow after rehearsals. Including Clarissa." She slammed the door only to open it again to snatch the pancakes up. She caught Terrence's knowing gaze. "Who am I kidding? I won't leave this to waste." She slammed the door one more time for good measure.

Chapter Three

Tom woke up the following morning, to the shrill sound of his cell phone ringing. It had to be his manager, the only person who would dare wake someone up at six in the morning without any care or consideration.

"Maurice," he growled into the phone.

"Turn on Channel 9. I'll call you back in five." The line went dead. Tom rolled his eyes tiredly. Maurice Doyle wasn't known for his manners, just his business savvy.

Tom did as he was told but all he saw was a commercial for dentures. He rolled over, snuggling down into his comforter, eyelids heavy with the need for sleep. He hadn't slept well, since he couldn't stop thinking about that insane interview. What was Trace even playing at? Humiliating that poor woman on television like that. What was he trying to accomplish besides making her look desperate and him like an unfeeling cad. Tom groaned at the memory of her retreating back as she fled the stage. She had really nice legs, though, and an amazing singing voice.

December Brown, huh? He'd have to Google her after the awards show he had to attend tonight.

"Last night on the 'Trace Randall Tonight' show, British actor Tom Elmswood and singer December Brown were the subjects of a matchmaking experiment gone sour." A female announcer's voice said. Tom bolted right up, raising the volume on the TV.

So this is what Maurice wanted him to see. 'The Morning Gossip' with Valerie Maldonado replayed the segment in all of its awkward glory. Tom winced at the look of mortification on December's face before she buried it in her hands. He watched himself whisper into her ear as it turned red. Tom felt a flutter in his stomach, as he saw her literally pull herself together on camera. Did she ever do any acting before? Because the way she tamped down her emotions and plastered on that smile was a thing of beauty.

"Trace Randall may have thought he was playing cupid but from the look of disinterest on the talented actor's face, the arrow definitely hadn't struck. Poor December, unlucky in love, but overflowing with talent." Valerie said before moving on to her daily doggy pampering segment.

Tom quickly changed the channel to MTV. He only caught the ending of their take on last night's show. "December Brown looked positively enamored by Tom Elmswood, only to have her obvious crush on him rubbed in her face, not a minute later. Will Tom ever ask her out? Probably not, but hey, I'd date you any day, December. Girl, you are scorching!" the mohawked VJ said with an overly dramatic wink.

Tom couldn't help himself. He kept switching channels to hear more opinions about the 'event'. He wanted to murder Trace. Every journalist at tonight's award show would be asking him about December and her text. The media made him out to be dispassionate and uninterested, which made him feel like the scum of the earth on top of it all. He'd never even heard of the woman before last night, why was this happening to him? Damn that Trace Randall.

Tom had tried to stay out of the media circus his entire career. He didn't date within the industry. He was always polite to the paparazzi and signed every autograph. He answered every question reporters asked him, and for the past five years, it had all worked out perfectly. Hell, he'd even been voted Sexiest Man and he wasn't even trying. Yanking on a t-shirt, Tom decided he needed a plan of action. His cell phone began ringing and he picked up instantly.

"Hello?"

"Did you see it? That little stunt has everyone talking about you!"

"I'm sorry, Maurice. I couldn't help it. Blame Trace Randall for this debacle."

"What debacle? This is gold. Free publicity, Tommy boy! My phone has been ringing off the hook since it aired last night!"

"You're not mad? It's tabloid fodder, Maurice..."

"Well, maybe in a week. But for now, we can spin this anyway we want to."

"We can? How?" Tom asked hesitantly.

"Tonight at the Critic's Awards, answer the questions any reporter asks. Be honest, but vague. Like you did last night."

"I can do vague since I haven't a clue about what's happening. Should I call December? I wonder how she's handling all of this..." Tom murmured worriedly.

"I'll get you her number later. But for now, just lay low. She's performing on the show tonight. Keep your distance until I can get in touch with her manager to see where her head's at. Got it?" His agent barked out in his gruff way.

"I suppose..." Tom didn't feel very assured, but Maurice was very good at his job so he had no choice but to trust him.

"Good. The limo will pick you up at four."

Once again the dial tone signaled the end of discussion. Maurice had an aversion to saying goodbyes and hellos. Tom slowly put his phone down and flopped back down on his bed. He suddenly felt bone tired. This was going to be a very long day.

Chapter Four

December rehearsed her butt off. Even her hard to please choreographer, Nathan Morris, was pleased with her dedication. She rarely showed such focus in rehearsals unless he'd threatened her with bodily harm. But not today; from the very start, she put her all plus even more, into learning the routine.

"Dee, that was fantastic. You're going to be phenomenal tonight." Nathan clapped a hand on her shoulder, forcing her to stand still.

"You should go rest up. The show starts in a few hours."

"What about my performance with Dante?" December panted, still out of breath but energized. She felt like she could take on the world. "Shouldn't we rehearse that too?"

"It's only a duet, honey. Don't be nervous. All you have to do is bop along to the beat and flirt with him when he moves around you on stage." Nate answered, tossing his gear into his gym bag. "I'll see you on stage. Laters."

December watched his retreating form with a frown. She had a few more hours to kill. She didn't want to think about yesterday so she wanted to be kept mind-numbingly busy. She hadn't even gone online just so she wouldn't have to know what people said about last night's show. She wanted zero distractions for today. Walking quickly to the door, she called her driver to pick her up. It would take Terrence at least two hours to get her looking presentable for tonight, right? That sounded like a plan. December's cell phone buzzed in her hand so she looked down to see Clarissa's name on the screen. Sighing deeply, she answered.

"Yes, Clarissa? What is it?" She kept her voice cold.

"You can't stay mad at me forever, you know." Her best friend said anxiously.

"Well I'm just going to have to give it a good ol' college try, now won't I?"

"I'm sorry, okay? I shouldn't have trusted Trace to handle that with tact and subtlety. It was my fault. Don't blame Terrence." Clarissa bleated.

"I didn't. I knew it was you and that butthead from the start."

"So you accept my apology then?" she asked, hope evident in her voice.

"What? No way. Also those pancakes weren't even up to IHOP's standard. I think there were real blueberries in there and you know how I feel about that." December shuddered. She might have said blueberry pancakes but she definitely just wanted the blueberry syrup the restaurant chain offered. There was nothing fruity in that fruit sauce. Just the way she liked it.

"Okay, how about tomorrow I'll bring them with me?"

"With sausage and scrambled eggs?"

"But of course."

"Alright. I might let you in, but don't count on it."

"Yay! You do love me."

"Uh huh."

"I really am sorry, babe. I swear I didn't know he was going to do that. I thought since it was only you and Tom as the guests, he'd maybe play a game and get you two talking. I didn't think he'd pull out that old text message."

"Ugh. I don't want to talk about it... but he smelled so good, C. And he was super nice and so freaking' gorgeous." December admitted, gushing and whining in one fell swoop.

"I know. I saw. That man is yummy. What did he whisper to you when your face was covered?"

"He said 'not to worry'. That 'the worst was over.' His lips were right on my ear! I don't know how I didn't just throw myself at him, screeching my love for him like a deranged animal."

"I was very impressed at that too. You seemed very calm and very into him."

"Really? Do you think he noticed? "

"Um..."

"He didn't notice, did he? I knew it. I should have screeched."

Clarissa giggled, "He would have definitely noticed that. But seriously, Dee, you didn't embarrass yourself one bit. Trace did that but you remained cool throughout. You could play this any way you want to now."

"What do you mean?" December knew that she was now talking to Clarissa's publicist side.

"This is spin control, babe. The press won't leave you alone until you give them something, you know that, right? So you can make it out to be just a little crush and laugh it off. Maybe a few tabloids will make stuff up to try to drag it out, but within the month it'll be old news. Or you can call Tom, apologize and do a couple of tweets back and forth so the fans know you're friends now. No hard feelings. You both get extra exposure, but on your own terms."

"I don't like using Twitter. The fact that I can only use so many words makes me feel like it's a test and I'll fail if I can't get it all in there just right. Also, I'm not too keen on this calling Tom business."

"What? Why?"

"I overheard him basically say that the thought of even having to date me was repulsive." So she embellished a little, big deal.

"You're probably exaggerating. But even so, he's still a jerk for even alluding to that. You are a total catch." Clarissa remarked.

"Yeah, yeah, so do I get out of this Tweeting thing or what?"

"Maybe. I'll call his people and see what's what first. I won't make the show tonight, but I'll see you first thing tomorrow. Any reporters ask that about your text, just blush and talk about the charity."

"Will do, Mon Capitan."

"Dork. Love you. Talk to you tomorrow."

"Love you too. Buhbye."

Halfway through the drive back to the hotel, Clarissa called again.

"Hi hi."

"Hey, just listen, there's a change of plans. I've arranged for your driver to take you straight to the arena building so you'll enter through the side door. The red carpet won't be set up yet so very few people will be milling around. Terrence is already on his way. After he's through with you, I arranged a short interview for you with Celebrity News. It's an exclusive agreement, so she won't be asking you about Tom. Like, at all. You'll simply talk at length regarding tonight's charity efforts. Answer all the other questions except for Tom stuff. If she asks, ignore her. But do it politely and bashfully. Two photographers will be allowed to take pictures of you and your dress for the fashion by-lines. Then you'll be ushered inside to your seat until it's time for you to perform. Afterwards you'll sneak out the back exit precisely at nine. Which is a full hour before anyone else will be allowed to leave. I've already briefed Damien to keep you on track." She directed briskly, sounding a lot less jovial than she did when they ended their previous call.

"Alright, but why the sudden change of plans?" December's eye twitched in worry. Clarissa only assigned her bodyguards for public events and concerts. Damien was the head of her security team back in New York. He rarely flew out to meet her anywhere unless she was on tour.

"Is this for my safety? Do I have another stalker? Oh God, is it the same one from before?" Her voice became shriller with each word.

"No, calm down. It's nothing like that. It's just a pre-emptive strike. I'll explain in the morning, until then do not under any circumstances watch the TV, listen to the radio, or go online." Clarissa's voice was confident enough that December believed her. She took a deep relaxing breath, steadying herself.

"OK. Do I still have to talk to Tom?"

"Hold that thought, sweets. For now, we'll let him deal with the fallout. "

"What fallout? There's more?"

"Do what I told you, December. I mean it."

"You know I will."

She'd learned from experience to heed Clarissa's warnings. It usually entailed something she would regret hearing about until Clarissa was able do damage control. December was more than happy to live in her carefully constructed bubble.

"Okay. Good. Just follow Damien's instructions and it'll all go smoothly. I'll call you tonight and explain everything. Bye."

"Talk to you later then." December stared at her phone blankly for a few seconds before slipping it back into her purse. She trusted Clarissa and Damien implicitly. Terrence however would not be happy since they rarely got along.

Damien of the giant rugged Australian stock and Terrence with his frail, wispy frame, were like oil and water. Or was it more like venom and bloodstreams? Either way it was not pretty when they had to be in the same room together for longer than an hour. At nearly 6'4" with sandy blond hair, emerald green eyes, and the poutiest, most kissable lips that was every woman's downfall, Damien Fimmel was a total stud. And he knew it with every long legged, thick-thighed stride. Therefore, he was more than a little arrogant and that was where Terrence stepped in, to tell him about himself. He bickered unmercifully while Damien baited him at each turn, since he apparently got a kick out of winding him up. For an ex-Navy Seal-turned-bodyguard, Damien was a pretty mellow guy. Meanwhile, for a man who went to fashion school and barely weighed one hundred and forty pounds soaking wet, Terrence was kind of a hothead.

December spotted Damien posed against the building as the town car finally rolled up to her new destination. By the time she stepped out of the automobile, he was by her side, sweeping her into a brisk but firm hug.

"Hey, short stuff." To Damien everyone was short, so December didn't mind one bit, especially when he flashed his megawatt smile her way. "It's good to see you again."

"It's good to see you too. How's Marilyn?" She asked following him inside.

"She's about to pop any day now. We're having a little girl," he told her proudly.

Probably everyone in the Tri-state area knew Damien and Marilyn were having a baby girl. But he looked so delighted, it was contagious. December cooed in happiness for him.

"Congratulations, Damien. You're going to be a fantastic Daddy." She said, finally telling him what she'd wanted to say all along.

"Thanks, Kitten, that means a lot to me. I mean it. I'm so nervous but excited." He grinned down at her, before his smile softened with sympathy. "So listen... I'm sorry about that guy. We saw it on TV last night."

"Oh well, it's the story of my life. Girl passively stalks guy. Girl gets drunk and texts traitorous talk show host. Boy thinks girl is vomitus." December deadpanned. Damien guffawed loudly despite himself and poked her lightly in the side, making her laugh.

"You're too good for him anyway. The man has the ultimate poker face. I doubt he even has emotions. Hell, he might even be a cyborg." He winked at her conspiratorially, and she beamed back in gratitude. December really loved her friends. They babied her like nobody's business, but she truly appreciated it.

"Alright, enough chit-chat. Let's get down to brass tacks here, Missy. You don't go anywhere without me. Clarissa must have pulled a lot of strings if she got you this kind of special treatment, so let's make her efforts worth it, yeah? I'll wait outside while you get ready. Terrence is already inside your dressing room. Yes, of course it has a shower. And yes, Clarissa does think of everything. I'll escort you to your seats, where you'll sit between Terrence and me. When it's time for your performances, we'll be waiting backstage for you." Damien instructed, as they strode further into the building.

"Got it. What about the photographs and interview?"

"I'll knock on your door in an hour and forty-five minutes, then take you to the enclosed red carpet area. It will be closed for at least fifteen minutes; therefore you get five, maybe ten minutes worth of photographs. Then I'll take you to a small seating area where you'll have a five minute interview. After that, it's the seats. Any questions?"

"Nope. I don't think you left anything out," she replied, committing his words to memory.

"Good. You'll thank us later for this, trust me."

"Famous last words?"

"Oi, just get in there." Damien rolled his eyes and playfully shoved her towards her dressing room door where Terrence awaited with open arms.

"Hey baby girl, ready for tonight?" Terrence asked once Damien shut the door behind her.

"Wait a minute. You two didn't say one mean word to each other. Is it that bad?" she asked anxiously, chewing on her bottom lip.

"To be honest, it's not. But the fallout with the press always makes everything seem so much worse. Especially in the beginning, so that's why you're getting the super sheltered treatment." Terrence admitted, honest as ever.

"That makes sense. But what about the banter? I miss the banter." December secretly breathed a sigh of relief. At least things hadn't gotten worse.

"He's going to be a dad. My crush is officially over." He dramatically slumped down on the styling chair in the middle of the room.

"Wait, you had a crush on him?" she asked, glad for the chance to focus on something else, although she actually was flabbergasted at Terrence's admission.

"Yes, dummy. Insults equal flirting? Hello, I was playing hard to get." Terrence explained, shocked she hadn't caught on ages ago.

"Well, sorry. You know I don't understand the subtleties of courtship," December remarked, sarcastically.

"Hush up, you." He laughed, handing her a toiletry bag "Go shower, it's through that little red door. We need to hurry."

An hour and half later, Damien knocked on the door, announcing it was time to wrap it up. December and Terrence emerged from the room two minutes later, all decked out for the occasion. Terrence in a snazzy suede-edged tan suit and December in a gauzy pale pink floor-length gown with a plunging sweetheart neckline, her hair done up in a loose chignon. Even Damien donned a black suit jacket over his white t-shirt, just for the occasion.

He whistled his appreciation. "December, you look wow. T-Dog, you done good."

Terrence's grip on her hand tightened. "Friend-zoned like you wouldn't believe." he hissed, despondently. She squeezed his hand back and rubbed his arm. Apparently her bad luck in love was catching. "Go on. I'll wait here. I need a minute alone."

"You know what we're going to do, Terr? We're going to have fun. We are not going to be sad. We're going to enjoy the hell out of tonight. Then we'll go back to the hotel and watch a terrible movie and probably sob until it's time to go to the airport. But first, there will definitely be dancing," December whispered fiercely into his ear. He nodded in agreement with unshed tears brimming in his eyes. She hugged him tightly, careful not to disrupt all of his hard work.

"Okay, the reporter you're talking to is Susannah Golden. She's been at Celebrity News for about two years and this is her big break. So be easy on her." Damien muttered quickly.

He took her arm once the photographers had all the images they needed and led her over to a nervous-looking woman with bleached blonde hair and a slightly manic smile. December vaguely recognized from her TV, while beside her stood a tall cameraman whose face remained hidden behind the large equipment he was focused on.

"Oh my, don't you look breath-taking. It's such a pleasure to meet you, December." They shook hands, as her smile got wider and more unhinged.

"Thank you so much for having me, Susannah." December replied, blushing at the compliment.

"Are you excited to be performing tonight?"

"Oh yes, this is the first time I'll be performing at the 'Critic's Favorites' Awards'. I'm just so nervous I might trip on stage and make a fool of myself." December admitted, grinning.

Susannah chuckled, "I'm sure you'll be fine. Who designed this gorgeous dress of yours?"

"This is a Terrence Mitchell Original. It's fantastic, isn't it?" December twirled around slightly.

Agreeing heartily, Susannah smoothly shifted the topic. "So we know you usually like to raise awareness about a different charity or foundation whenever you perform. What cause will you be promoting tonight?"

"I'm donating eighty percent of the proceeds from my latest single and tonight's appearance fee to something that's close to my heart, The Philadelphia Children's Home."

"Is that an orphanage?"

"Yes, it's the place I called home for the first ten years of my life. The building needed repairs, so I've decided to completely renovate it to make it a real home for the kids who live there. A home is a source of pride and belonging for people, whether it's a house with a family or an orphanage. These children need something to hold on to, and I'm going to try my very best to give them that." December expounded.

Susannah's eyes softened as she listened to December's impassioned speech. "That's very admirable. It's no wonder that you're such an inspiration to your fans."

"I don't know about all of that, but I do know that I'm in a position to help as many people as I can, and I love doing it." December spoke with heartfelt sincerity.

The two women continued chatting for a few more minutes about her upcoming projects and general industry talk, when Susannah suddenly began to fidget nervously. She looked incredibly reluctant to ask the question that was written on her index card prompt.

"So December you're usually very private about your dating life but since that's all changed after last night... Is there a special someone waiting at home for you or are you hoping Tom Elmswood will call?"

December smiled wanly at her, and redirected the subject. "Can I just thank my fans for being so supportive and wonderful each and every day? I love you all."

Damien sensed that this was her way of ending the interview before it went awry. He motioned for the cameraman to wrap up filming and led December away after she said her goodbyes.

"So, how did I do?"

"Great. We just have to make it through your two songs and we'll be home in no time."

"Oh, thank God. I've had enough of sunny LA and I've only been outside for like ten minutes. "

Chapter Five

Tom stepped out of his limo into the throngs of barely contained paparazzi. Hundreds of camera flashes and the buzzing sound of many people talking at once was something he'd become accustomed to so much so that his eyes adjusted almost instantaneously. He smoothed down his classically cut, tailored tuxedo and turned to face the mob of journalists, photographers and cameramen lined along the length of the red carpet. Everyone seemed to be shouting for his attention, to ask him a question or for him to face this way or that. He plastered on a smile on his face and prepared himself for the oncoming barrage.

"Tom, did you really say December Brown was disgusting?"

Wait. What? He wasn't expecting that. Not at all.

"Tom, did you say she was repulsive to her face or behind her back?" another reporter shouted at him.

"I don- I don't know what you're talking about?" He asked, visibly confused.

"Can you confirm that you said 'December Brown was the last woman you'd ever date even if the world ended today'?"

"Okay. That's just laughable. But I'm still lost. Can someone please tell me what's going on here?" Tom was baffled. Maurice was probably going to rip him a new one for not sticking with the plan but he was clearly at a loss for this line of questioning.

"Sources have revealed that yesterday after the "Trace Randall Tonight" show, you said that December was repulsive and un-dateable. Can you confirm?" A tall brunette lady journalist clarified, glaring at him all the while.

"I said no such thing. I'm sorry to tell you, but your sources are wrong." Tom responded confidently.

"So you didn't have December in tears after you said and I quote, 'The very idea of being with her makes me sick to my stomach?'" asked a stocky, nondescript looking bald man towards the back.

Tom faltered, the words of denial stuck in his throat. While he hadn't used those exact words, he did say something along those lines to his handler, Patrick, in the dressing room after the show. Whoever overheard him must have told her, which in turn had made her cry. Tom truly felt like pond scum. He had to find a way to make it right with her.

"I never said those words exactly. December seems like a very sweet woman. I would never."

"You would never what? Date her?" The crowd went into an uproar making his words sounds more and more like an insult.

"No, I meant I would never say something like that about her. Or make her cry. I'm truly sorry if that is actually the case." Tom declared honestly. He walked off towards the seating area after that, lost in his thoughts.

Tom spotted her in the audience two rows in front of him, sandwiched between two men. A tall, burly blond and a shorter man with a dark brown complexion. He wouldn't have even recognized her if it wasn't for the people around him whispering how 'December was so brave for showing up tonight.' She didn't seem miserable or dejected from where he was sitting. Then again he was staring at the back of her head. But for all intents and purposes, the three seemed delighted to be there. She whispered animatedly to the shorter man until the behemoth tapped her on her opposite shoulder causing her to look in the wrong direction. Once she realized that it was him, she swatted him on the arm, causing him to laugh.

Tom stared at the threesome intently, both willing and not willing her to turn around and look at him. Perhaps a wave or some sort of gesture to let him know that she didn't think poorly of him. But she didn't. And Tom couldn't help but feel a little disappointed as the lights in the cavernous auditorium dimmed down, signifying the start of the awards show. It hadn't even occurred to him that she might not have known that he was present.

If it wasn't for December and her friend in the light-colored suits seated dancing and exaggerated lip-synching to the musical acts and over enthusiastic clapping for every single nominee, Tom would have been bored to tears. Apparently, the large man felt the same since he was in stitches every time the duo started up.

Tom wished he could have changed his seat closer to hear them or at least see them better, but instead he resigned himself to memorizing the curve of her shoulders and the way her dark tendrils of hair rested against her neck. He told himself it was boredom since he knew absolutely nothing about her except that she seemed to be more trouble than she was worth at the moment. Tom was definitely going to Google her tonight. He'd planned on doing it earlier today but he ended up busy dealing with a billion phone calls from his entire public relations team. And yet they'd all neglected to tell him that he was a social pariah.

So after being told off in a hundred ways for several hours, he'd switched off his cell phone and gone for a swim in the hotel's pool. Tom realized now that he'd forgotten to turn it back on and that's probably why he was caught unaware. He contemplated on pretending to go to the restroom then sneaking out but decided against it since he was presenting 'Best Supporting Actress in a Drama'. Not to mention that one of his movies was nominated for 'Best Lighting' or something to that effect. Tom knew his presence for that wasn't necessary but he wanted to show solidarity to the movie crew that had worked so hard.

Tom looked up in time to see December and her friends shuffle out of the aisle and quickly walk towards the backstage. Was she presenting an award as well or maybe performing? Tom wondered to himself. He had to admit she had a lovely voice even though he was only half listening last night. He was preoccupied with preparing himself for Trace's zany line of questioning. Unfortunately, there was no way for him to prep himself for that disaster.

A few minutes later, the lights dimmed once again. The host for the evening announced that Dante and December

Brown would be performing his award winning song, before music poured through the filled amphitheater. Dante, a handsome Latino man began crooning a sultry love song that Tom had never heard before. It wasn't bad but it wasn't his usual taste. He was more of a classic rock type of guy. And when he said classic he meant classic. If it was popular after Queen or Journey's time chances were he was unfamiliar with it. Aerosmith was probably the most recent band he started listening to.

But when December joined in with her stronger, more melodic voice, Tom definitely paid rapt attention this time. She looked mesmerizing in her nearly see-through pale pink dress. It fit her body like a glove, accentuating her curves and her flawless caramel skin. He watched as she danced coyly around Dante while they harmonized. Then he glared when Dante seductively serenaded her during his solo parts of the song. And when he pulled her hand to his chest during the final notes, Tom scowled into the darkness of the theatre. What kind of name was Dante anyway? He looked short. He was probably short. Tom figured he could take him in a fight. Then he realized that he was possibly losing his mind. This was not the Tom Elmswood way. He didn't become jealous over a woman he hardly knew, who probably hated him now anyway. He was forever cool, like James Bond cool. At least that's what he told himself. However in that particular moment, his palms were sweaty and he really wanted to kick Dante right in the seat of his blindingly white suit. And yet despite his sudden feelings of brief animosity, he found himself getting to his feet and applauding along with the rest of the crowd.

The trio later came back to their seats much to Tom's relief. He spent another thirty minutes staring at the back of their heads, as if it was the best show in the world. He gathered from the way, the skinnier man fussed and fiddled with December's hair that he was at the very least her hair stylist. He also deduced that the Norse god who was constantly on alert and very protective of her was her bodyguard. Unless he was her boyfriend. Wait, that couldn't be true because she had a no longer secret crush on Tom himself. After panicking for a second, he smiled once he remembered that little tidbit. But then...what if Blondie was interested her but she hadn't realized it yet? Tom's stomach flip-flopped in a sudden case of despair.

The light in his self-made tunnel appeared in the form of a glint of gold on the big man's left hand. Tom audibly sighed in relief. He silently thanked his mother for bestowing him the gift of wedding band hunting. After years of her dragging him on husband scouting excursions, Tom could now see an engagement or wedding ring from a mile away. And that wasn't even exaggerating much. By the time his cast mate nudged him to go backstage, he was exhausted from the roller coaster ride of emotions he put himself through. Who knew that staring at the back of someone's head could be so riveting? Tom strode purposefully through the aisle hoping that December would finally notice his existence, but he didn't want to turn around in case he appeared too eager.

Chapter Six

The second Tom's name was called two strong hands on either side of December gripped hers. She was grateful for their support, particularly because she wasn't a hundred percent sure that she wouldn't have run screaming out of the building. He looked so yummy in his tuxedo. Black was definitely his color. His lightly sun kissed skin framed by inky black hair stood in stark contrast to his glacier blue eyes.

When he played the role of a self-indulgent vampire, a few years earlier, his fame rocketed. Between his cultured accent, richly masculine voice, and that perfectly perfect mouth, ovaries around the world combusted. His face was the stuff of legend. If Damien was a stud, then Tom Elmswood was a babe. And December didn't regret a thing, even after all the kerfuffle. Damn him for being an idiot. That part she regretted. Not to mention, him finding out about her crush and her looking like a total dingbat. Yeah, she could do without all of that. December clutched Terrence's hand tightly, as Tom did the introductions for the nominations. That voice of his could make butter melt in the Arctic tundra, no additional heat source needed.

"I could see why you'd crush on him so hard. Damn, he's fine." Terrence whispered, grasping her sweaty palm tighter.

"You could say that again. I wouldn't kick him out of bed." Damien agreed, whistling the loudest catcall known to man.

"Oh Jesus." Terrence murmured before the three of them burst into hysterical giggles. "Don't look. Don't look. He's staring directly at us!"

December slid straight down in her seat. If she went any further she'd be on the floor.

"Why must I look like a spaz every time he notices me?" She groaned.

"Who wants to bet they caught that on camera?" Damien pondered aloud. December slouched down further at the thought.

Tom couldn't help but grin at December and her friends' antics. It would certainly be in every celebrity magazine coming out within the week. When he'd sauntered back to his seat, purposefully slowing down the closer he got to the trio's row, she refused to make eye contact with him but the boys didn't show the same kind of reluctance. Instead they winked and gave him thumb's ups, even as she elbowed them both hard. Tom didn't even mind sitting through the next hour of the show. He was positively elated. He planned on catching up with them after the show ended. The fact that she stayed slouched down in her seat the entire time only encouraged him.

Tom watched curiously as they left for backstage again. Was she going to perform again? She must have been exhausted. Flying from Vancouver to Los Angeles had left him feeling drained and out of sorts most of the day, so he could only imagine how she had to be feeling. She couldn't possibly have gotten much rest because of rehearsals and everything that entailed. Tom found himself worrying about her well-being. He didn't really understand these newfound sentiments but he really wanted to talk to her. Perhaps they could have brunch or something before he left, Tom thought himself. He was going to fly back to NYC tomorrow afternoon. Eager to be back in his own bed, but loathe to not enjoy Los Angeles for at least an afternoon, he'd taken a later flight than Maurice wanted him to.

When the pulsating tempo of a new song started to play, Tom's eyebrows raised in surprise. While he wasn't familiar with her work as yet, he didn't peg her for doing fast dance music. He assumed she only sang ballads and the like. She strutted on stage in a pair of wet look leather pants and matching midriff baring top, sporting dramatic makeup as the music changed into a more intense crescendo. Tom was taken aback as she danced seductively along with the other dancers, singing a somewhat suggestive, definitely empowering song.

December moved gracefully to the beat, belting out notes in a throaty tone that sent chills down Tom's spine. She was just full of surprises wasn't she? How did she go from the demure girl who blushed at just about anything to the sexy vixen on stage? Tom wasn't complaining in the least. He simply wondered if this performance came with a cigarette, for after. The crowd erupted in applause as she bowed and smiled gratefully at them. Their eyes met for the briefest of moments before she was off the stage. That was the last he saw of her for the rest of the evening. Tom waited eagerly for her return but their seats remained empty all the way to the end.

Nathan swung her around in celebration as soon as they'd run backstage "Oh my God, you were amazing. I'm so proud of you."

"Thanks Nate, but all the praise should go to you. You're the choreographer. Sorry, I mean the genius." December bowed to his greatness.

"Why thank you! I think I shall take all of that praise." Nate said, giving her another tight squeeze before turning to congratulate the rest of his team of backup dancers. Terrence and Damien were motioning for her to leave, so December waved to everyone and quickly followed them to where the car awaited. She hadn't even had a chance to change her clothes so she still wore those hellish leather pants that stuck to her skin. There would be tears when she took them off, thanks to the LA heat.

"Clarissa booked us all on a flight to NYC at two in the morning. That means we have at least four hours to rest up. Do you mind if I crash with you guys? I literally got off the plane and went straight to the theatre." Damien sat on her left, squishing them both into the right side of the town car's backseat. It was safe to say everyone involved regretted not requesting a limo instead.

"Of course, Damien. We have the presidential suite so there's more than enough room." December replied, avoiding Terrence's imploring look. "You can have Terry's room. He can bunk with me." Terrence literally deflated with relief at her words.

"Yes. Yes, good idea. We wanted to have a slumber party anyway, right Dee?" Damien hadn't seemed to notice any hesitation or Terrence's weirdly stiff words.

"Awesome. You guys are the best. I need to get as much rest as I can before the baby arrives, you know?"

Once they'd arrived back to December's hotel room, Terrence fled to her bedroom. She sighed deeply, showing Damien to his new room as well as gathering Terrence's belongings to take with her.

"Is Terrence alright? He was pretty quiet all evening. He didn't even threaten to shave my head. I'm not feeling the love." Damien inquired, sprawling out on the king-sized bed.

December kept her head down, pretending to be very interested in packing away her friend's things into his overnight bag. She had to be careful about what she said in order to preserve the delicate equilibrium that was already in place between the two men. Also she really hated being caught in the middle.

"Um I think he was just feeling under the weather." she mumbled, weakly.

"He seemed fine when you two were acting like fools." He remarked, sitting up to lean up against the headboard.

"Oh you know how that is. He was just caught up in all the... uh revelry?" she ditched the idea of zipping up the bag and decided to leg it out of there, as is.

"Have a seat, Miss Brown. We need to play catch up." Damien demanded, somewhat menacingly.

"I'm pretty tired and Terrence might nee-" December began but he cut her off.

"Sit down, December." He urged, patting the mattress beside him.

"Stupid Terrence. Yellow bellied chicken." she grumbled as she shuffled over to perch at the edge of the bed.

"Can I braid your hair?" Damien muttered, softly.

"What?" December gave him a funny look.

"What? Nothing... So tell me why Terrence is acting different. And don't you lie to me, little girl."

"Little? We're two years apart, sir." she huffed.

"Okay please tell me. It's weird now. I'm so used to him joking with me." he pleaded, moving closer. She knew he was crowding her on purpose since not only was she a bad liar, she also became easily flustered during confrontations. This was one of the main reasons Clarissa kept such tight reins with media exposure.

"You called that joking? I mean things are different now, you know? You're going to be a dad. So maybe he's just treating you like a grown up." December rationalized. It wasn't a total lie. She just omitted a few things.

"I thought he had a crush on me? What happened with that?" Damien asked, nonchalantly as he twirled a lock of her hair.

There was loud thud in the living room area, and then a door slammed. Apparently, Terrence heard and was just as shocked as she was. Taking a deep breath, December sought to remain impassive for everyone's sake.

"Crush? On you? Ha. You know what? These pants are starting to chafe. I need to go change. See you in the morning." she said all of this in a rush, disregarding the look of amusement on Damien's face, as she high tailed it out of the room.

"Tell Terrence good night for me. We'll talk more over breakfast." he called out after her, obviously trying not to laugh.

In the safety of her private room, December found Terrence face down on the floor. She sighed deeply. "Can I just change out of this leather outfit first, before I join you?"

He mumbled something that she took for agreement as she slipped into the en suite bathroom. Clad in her pajamas, she crawled over to his still prostrate body, a short while later.

"Sugar pie, you can't lay there all night. You can sulk just as good on the bed." Terrence turned his face to the side and stared at her with the saddest brown eyes she'd ever seen

"It's more pathetic this way. Just kill me now because I can never face him again"

"He didn't seem to mind too much. I think he's known for some time." She said as she began to ease his jacket off slowly, one arm at a time, without any assistance from him.

"That's what makes it worse." he opined, turning his head away from her so she couldn't see his tears. Tossing his jacket on the chair a few feet from her, she laid down next to him, cuddling close.

"I bet there are dust mites in this carpet."

"We're talking about me still, December."

"Oh I know. I was just wondering if Damien is really worth getting a dust mite infestation over." she replied, blandly.

Terrence snorted, "Ugh I think I got some up my nose. I hate you." December chuckled, hugging him once they both sat up.

"It was a pipe dream, I know. I mean he was married when we met him. I really shouldn't feel this bad but I can't help it." he explained, dejectedly.

"Why shouldn't you? Damien is freaking' hot."

"You're not helping, Dee."

"Wait, hear me out. This is coming from experience okay? Like current experience. Sobbing over gorgeous guys not liking us back makes sense. We're human and this is a major loss."

"Ugh, I really thought you were going to say something wise for a moment there but then... nothing." Terrence said, rolling his eyes, dramatically. December pinched him, giggling.

"Honestly, it did sound more profound in my head. Seriously though, think of it this way, now it's all out in the open. You can't get any lower than this. So now all you can go is up."

"That's both depressing and accurate. I wish we had ice cream to celebrate this sudden logic."

"Oh God, yes! That would help." December moaned, standing up. She leaned over to pull Terrence to his feet.

"So Tom seemed into you tonight..." he said wiggling his eyebrows suggestively. December glared at him.

"Maybe you misheard him last night?" Terrence added gently.

"What didn't Clarissa want me to see before the show? Did he say something worse about me that she had to protect me from?" she asked suddenly, switching tactics. Since apparently steely silence wasn't going to work.

"Not really. Remember that thing you told me about last night? When he said that thing about dating you?"

"How I was the grossest person ever and he hated me? Yeah I remember ..." Terrence rolled his eyes at her.

"Well someone spilled it to the press and now they're foaming at the mouth over it."

December looked stricken. "What? Who would do that? Why would anyone do that? Do you think it was it Tom?"

"It wasn't Tom. I mean like why would he? It would only make him look bad, right?"

"Yeah that's true. Then who could it be? We didn't even talk to anyone after I overhead him last night." she pondered thoughtfully.

"Oh my God, I think I know who told." Terrence gasped.

"Really? Who?"

"The driver. The one from last night. It wasn't Ricky like we normally have when we're here in Los Angeles. I noticed last night but I didn't think..." Terrence reflected.

"So he heard my whole melt down" She whispered horrified. "I guess I have to talk to Tom now after all, don't I?"

Terrence nodded "You have to explain what happened and apologize."

"I'll do it tomorrow first thing. Right now though, I have the worst headache." She crawled under the comforter to sulk.

Chapter Seven

Oddly depressed, Tom went straight back to his hotel after the awards' ceremony finished. He thought about going to an after party that his cast mates were attending, but his heart wasn't in it.

Instead he took off his tux, slipped into his lounge wear, logged onto YouTube and did a search for December Brown. Doubtless, she was immensely talented and after watching every one of her official videos that was listed, he grew more and more enamored by the idea of her. She was everywhere and sang everything from her original music to covers of classics. How in the world did he ever miss her?

Nevertheless, it wasn't until he saw an uploaded recording of her singing informally at a small high school in Nebraska that he felt a weird stirring in his chest. He felt like the Grinch did when his heart grew twice the size. He wanted to see her again, to get to know her, to redo that whole first meeting so he could actually pay attention this time. Wearing faded jeans and a silly t-shirt with her hair loosely falling around her shoulders, she sat laughing and joking around with a group of teenagers, is when December looked her prettiest to him. The kids begged her to sing something to them and she blushed like she always did, but even on the somewhat blurry camera phone, you could see plain as day that she was thoroughly enjoying herself. That she wouldn't have denied them anything they'd ask of her that day. Singing along to an acoustic guitar, she launched into his favorite song of all time. Her strong, clear voice made his heart skip a beat.

It was as if she was singing straight to him and Tom realized, without a shadow of a doubt, that this was his new favorite version of the song. He had to call her. He needed to talk to her and clear up all this crazy stuff going on.

He dialed up Maurice and explained to him what he needed. After Maurice told him off about time differences, and agreed to make the call, he paced. He wasn't an overly anxious kind of guy but the idea of talking to her made him so. It was an excited sort of nervousness that threatened to make him go for a jog just to exercise some of it out of his system. And he might have done it too, if Maurice hadn't called back just in time.

"You owe me for this. Her agent, Clarissa Gregory, didn't want to do it since you've screwed things up so royally. And you don't want to get her on that woman's bad side, trust me. But I promised her a favor since you wanted this so bad." Maurice groused.

"Thanks so much. Seriously, Maurice, whatever you want, just name it."

His humor-less agent actually laughed for once. "Man, I never thought I'd see the day. Anyway, tell me how it goes in case I need to clean up your mess again. Bye."

Tom stared at his phone suspiciously. Maurice Doyle had actually said a human goodbye to him. It was definitely a day of firsts.

It wasn't even ten yet but both men were fast asleep. Their soft snores threatened to lull December to slumber, but her fretfulness denied her rest. She was grateful for Clarissa's efficiency in keeping the media issues at bay but knew in the end she'd still have to admit her part in the rumor mill to Tom

Elmswood of all people. Maybe karma was on vacation since things kept going from awkward to downright humiliating at a rapid pace. This was the reason she was single. All this dating drama was too much for her to bear. And she wasn't even dating anyone, for Pete's sake.

Her cell phone began buzzing on the nightstand table beside her head, so she quickly snatched it up. She didn't recognize the number but it was a New York area code and she never could resist answering an unknown call, much to her friends' chagrin. Sure, she'd learned her lesson numerous times but still she picked up.

"Hello?" December whispered into her phone, trying not to wake up Terrence, who thankfully hadn't stirred.

"What kind of name is December anyway?" Tom blurted out. He cringed even though he was all alone in his hotel room.

"Um, who is this?" She asked, warily, tiptoeing into the living room area.

"I am so sorry. I don't know why I said that. Can we start again? "He said apologetically. Tom could practically feel her eyes narrow.

"Is this a telemarketer?" She responded, suspiciously.

"No it's Tom. Tom Elmswood." Such a long bout of silence held the line that he thought maybe she'd hung up on him.

"Oh sorry, I forgot to answer. Hi, Tom" December replied meekly.

"Hi, December." He smiled goofily at the blank pastel colored wall in front of him.

"I was going to call you tomorrow." she whispered.

"Were you?"

"Yes becau-"

"Why are you whispering?" Tom interrupted.

"Oh. The boys are asleep. I didn't want to wake them." December explained.

"But it's still so early..."

"We have an early flight."

"Ah I see. And the boys are... your sons?" He asked, casually.

"What? No, they're my friends. The two idiots who were with me tonight."

"Oh yes, the Adonis..." he pondered, knowingly.

December giggled throatily, "That would be Damien, my bodyguard. He gets that a lot."

"I bet." Tom sniffed, causing her to laugh harder. He liked the sound of it. "You were amazing tonight, by the way"

"Thank you." She said, brightly. Her voice was so breathy, it gave him tingles.

"I know I'm a fool for not hearing any of your songs before but I assumed you only sang ballads or something. I didn't expect your second act at all. It was so..."

"So what?" she prompted.

"It was so brazen."

"Brazen..." she repeated as if she were testing the word out.

"Yes. Oh God, did that sound bad? I meant it in a good way." he asked anxiously.

"No not at all. I've just never been called brazen before. I like it."

"Good." He sighed relieved. "I have to be careful these days since I seem to keep putting my foot in my mouth."

"Tom, I'm so sorry about all of this. I truly didn't know Trace was going to do that, and I definitely didn't know that the limo driver was eavesdropping on my conversation so he could sell it to the press." She spoke so rapidly her words began to jumble together. Tom wasn't a hundred percent sure he'd heard it all once she stopped.

"Sorry. I got the words Trace and limo. Can you repeat it all? Only slower?"

After listening to her repeated speech, he chuckled. "I think the universe could tell that you didn't plan to be side-lined by Mr. Randall's botched attempt at matchmaking. A little subtlety goes a long way, sometimes, don't you think?"

"Definitely. But still I needed to apologize for that. And my inappropriate text message, I was drunk and it was New Year's Eve and...sorry!"

"Don't be. It was sent privately. He's the one that made it public."

"I guess..."

"Can I ask where the limo driver got the idea that I thought you were disgusting?"

"I'll give you the short version. I was talking to Terrence, the other guy from tonight, about the fact that after Trace's show, I went to find you to commiserate but instead overheard you talking to someone. I hadn't meant to listen in but I heard something that upset me to which I repeated to Terrence and the driver overheard." December recanted with her eyes squeezed shut in mortification.

Tom stayed quiet for a moment too long so she had enough time to think of her new life as a recluse in a cave somewhere in the Himalayas.

"I never said or thought you were disgusting. Or horrible or any version of that." Tom finally replied, sympathetically.

"Oh."

"I was mainly upset at the idea of being forced into a publicized romance just because of some heavy handed ploy. I mean it was the first time we'd ever met and we don't even know each other..." He explained.

"That's true."

"But I'd like to get to know you now. It would be on our own terms, of course." December was at a loss for words.

"December? Are you still there?"

"Oh sorry, I forgot to respond again." He laughed at that.

"That's alright. So where do you live, December Brown?" Her brain nearly turned to mush at the way he said her name in that voice of his.

70

"First you thought I had children, now you don't even know what state I reside in? Didn't you Google me?" She teased, surprising herself at her flirty response.

"Sorry not yet, I only YouTube'd you. I'd rather ask you directly though. Perhaps over dinner sometime?"

"Err, what?" She must have heard wrong. There was no way he'd said what she thought he'd said.

"Will you have dinner or lunch with me?" Oh God, he did. Where were friends to urge her on when she needed them?

"I live in Manhattan." She said dumbly, answering his earlier question in an effort to stall. December really hated making social plans. Even if it was with the man of her dreams.

"Really? Oh that's fantastic. So do I. Where exactly?" he asked excitedly.

"Eighty-Fourth and York Avenue. What about you?"

"Wow, I wouldn't have pegged you for an Upper East Sider. I was thinking somewhere trendy."

"I like it quiet and unassuming. People don't bother you much there. Let me guess, you live in Midtown right?" December and Terrence had long ago come up with a theory about how most hot single guys seemed to reside in Midtown, Manhattan.

"Great guess. I mostly live out of my luggage, to be honest. I'm still trying to find my home."

"Aw, that's so sad."

"You just aww'd me. That's really cute."

"Bzzz... I think the line is breaking up." She quipped.

Tom laughed. "Have dinner with me. I'll be back in the city by tomorrow evening. I'll call you then okay?"

"Maybe."

"Maybe is good. I can work with maybe. It was great speaking with you, December. Sweet dreams."

"Same to you, Tom. Goodnight. Have a safe flight."

"You too. Bye."

After he hung up, she made sure the call was completely disconnected, then jumped up and down in silent jubilation. She turned to go back to bed only to find both Damien and Terrence smiling at her knowingly.

"Somebody has a boyfriend." They sang out. She turned beet red and flopped face down on the couch.

Chapter Eight

Eleven o'clock the next morning found December back in NYC, snoring soundly in her own bed.

"I know you have a doorman, but you should still lock your door." Clarissa whispered loudly into her ear. She woke up screaming bloody murder.

"Ugh, I hate it when you do that. Why can't you be normal?" December whined, willing her heartbeat to slow down. Her fight or flight adrenaline mode was trying to give her a heart attack first thing in the morning. She glared at her best friend with her bone straight golden hair, dark green eyes and high cheekbones and wanted to smack her right in the bubble gum pink lips.

"Uh huh, well, guess who brought you the blueberry syrup that she promised you?" Clarissa kicked off her expensive high heeled boots and climbed into bed beside her.

"Oh you do love me!" December exclaimed, giving Clarissa big wet smooch on the cheek.

"I do. I do. Now a little birdie told me that a certain gorgeous actor called you last night."

"Was that little birdie a 5'10" nosey queen?"

"More like a 6'4" gossiping Aussie."

"Ugh, Damien! That big mouth. Well guess what? He knew Terrence had a crush on him all along."

"I know. I called Terrence this morning and he told me the whole sad tale. Now don't try to change the subject, woman. I want details."

"What details? It was just a phone call." She said, shrugging.

"Oh yeah? So why are you grinning like an idiot?"

"Shut up. I'm not grinning. I'm smirking."

"With a wide toothy grin? Ha! No, you like him and he likes you. Maybe Trace wasn't so wrong after all."

"No, Trace was still wrong. And I hope he buys a bag of M&Ms' and it turns out it was a bag of sour Skittles. With no refunds. And that's all the money he had in his pocket so he can't buy anything else. I curse him... Skittles."

Clarissa giggled at her childishness. "So did Tom ask you out?"

"Kind of"

"Uh huh so that's a yes. Will you actually go out with him?"

"Maybe."

"OK so that's a no. Well, why not?"

Clarissa knew her entirely too well. They'd been best friends since 9th grade, so there was very little they didn't know about one another. From embarrassing adolescent shenanigans to nearly thirty 'they ought to know better', tomfoolery. Most of the time, Clarissa even knew December better than she knew herself. She knew that December had a gift that had to be shared with the world and that with the power that comes with being famous, December would wield it wisely. Except that on her own, without being dragged kicking and screaming, her gift would never see the light of day. So Clarissa, forever ambitious and prone to shrewdness, with just a dash of tyrannical ruler tendencies to spice things up, made that gift into a brand.

She protected December, with all the fierceness of a lioness, from the harsher aspects of fame so that she could just enjoy her music and revel in her generous nature. While she happily fought, scratched, bargained and sometimes threatened within the industry to keep it all together. It was hard, tireless work but Clarissa loved every minute of it. Being known as "The Destroyer" certainly had its perks. With that being said Clarissa was more than aware that when December said "maybe," that it usually meant not really, but she wanted to hear what the latest excuse was going to be this time.

"Publicity." December stated, while fidgeting. Clarissa fought with all her might not to roll her eyes. She failed abysmally.

"Really? That's the reason you're going to give me? Okay I'll bite. Elaborate, please."

"Well he wants to get back into the public's good graces. So making nice with me would do that. All he'd have to do is trot me out somewhere, make sure the paparazzi are conveniently there to take pictures. Then tada! He's no longer a social pariah." December explained, carefully avoiding eye contact.

"Alright I'll hand it to you. That is actually a pretty sound reason to not go out with him. It's crap of course, but very realistic."

"It's not crap. I swear, I don't him trust one bit. He was a little too smooth. What with those sexy dulcet tones and his interest..." She stared off dreamily.

"He's interested because you're wonderful, you ass! Anyway tell me everything he said."

December happily repeated the entire conversation to her. Clarissa listened intently, swooning at all the appropriate moments, while plotting her next move.

Tom barely made it through his door when his house phone began ringing. He dropped his luggage haphazardly in the front hallway and dove for the phone.

"Hello? Tom speaking."

"She's not going to go out with you."

"What? Who is this?"

"December is not going to go out with you." The female caller clarified

"What? Why not? "He asked aghast.

"She's a pain in the ass that's why."

"This is Clarissa, isn't it?"

"Duh. Anyway, she's her own worst enemy and she thinks you're only asking her out for the public's approval."

"You're joking?" Tom said in disbelief. He'd thought he'd made his intentions crystal clear during their phone conversation.

"I wish I was."

"So what should I do? I'd really love to see her." Clarissa smiled to herself, he was already hooked.

"Okay here's the plan. Go to her place for coffee."

"Will she be okay with that?"

"Don't worry about that. I'll handle that part. Just go visit her, make it casual and she'll relax a bit, then maybe she'll take you seriously."

"I'll need her address."

"That's the spirit."

Chapter Nine

Tom arrived at the address Clarissa gave him, at the time she'd expressly told him to go at. He trusted that Clarissa wouldn't turn out to be another Trace, blundering through matchmaking at warp speed. The car pulled up to a newly renovated high rise building on a pretty tree lined block. It was much different from his neighborhood, with its increasingly high buildings and lack of anything green. God, he could even hear birds on this street. He would bet there was even a quaint little park within walking distance. Tom accepted that he was a little bit envious.

He spoke to the doorman as per the instructions, who expected him. The only part of plan he deviated from was stopping to buy a couple of éclairs from his favorite bakery since they were meant to be having coffee. He was suffering from that nervous excitement again. Even the elevator ride to the tenth floor was taking too long for his taste. Tom took a deep breath then knocked on her door.

"Come in. The door's unlocked." December called out from somewhere in the large apartment.

He was overwhelmed by the feeling of home when he stepped into the foyer. Deep browns and gold with splashes of rich purples and turquoise enveloped him like a welcoming embrace, inviting him to unwind on one of the plush-looking sectional sets or to pad around in heavy woolen socks on a cold, rainy day where pajamas were the only clothes that seemed appropriate. It was an odd feeling to feel, as if he'd waited all his life to get there and it hadn't disappointed.

"Okay I know you dislike Manischewitz, but it's really the only wine I actually like drinking. I really hate the other stuff. It tastes a bit like hell- Oh. Tom. Hi." She stopped in astonishment.

His lips quirked into a smile at the sight of her standing there with her hair braided in two raggedy pigtails.

"Hi, December."

"You're not Clarissa." She said, stupidly. She hated surprises. Especially manipulative surprises, and so close after Trace's, it was enough to overtake her excitement of having Tom right in front of her.

"No." he replied, still smiling.

"But she told you to come over right?" Already knowing the answer, December sighed inwardly, accepting defeat. She would have threatened Clarissa with certain death, but she'd done that already and still she meddled. All she wanted was a quiet night in with her bestie.

"Yes." His smile wilted slightly at how visibly displeased she was. He figured something like this might happen, regardless of Clarissa's assurances, so he tried not to be offended. Tom knew all too well that playing with people like pawns tended to yield less than positive responses at times.

"Oh."

"Indeed."

She visibly shook herself from her stupor, and unconsciously started to unwind her sloppy plaits. A gorgeous man at your door, who wouldn't want to try to salvage their appearance?

"Since you're already here, come on in. Please." Tom's tentative smile widened, in relief at her invitation.

"I feel like a vampire. You've invited me in, there's no going back."

"That's not a comforting thought in the least, Tom." she retorted, dryly. Normally she'd have been guffawing like a maniac since he was obviously trying to alleviate the tension. Her dream guy was right in front of her, but all she wanted to do was smack someone.

"Sorry. I'm a little nervous." He said, still standing in her doorway, like a lost puppy. December took pity on him. Shaking her head in dismay, she walked over and closed the front door behind him.

"Don't be. Make yourself comfortable. Would you like something to drink?" December's words were reassuring but her manner was still distant at best. She knew it wasn't his fault but he was there and she was nothing if not temperamental.

"Are you upset with me?" he hovered close to her, trying to catch her eye.

"No I'm not upset with you." She said, honestly. She should have been over the moon that he was in her house, looking incredibly handsome in his navy blue coat, all buttoned up from the cold.

"Clarissa?" He guessed helpfully, as she took his coat. She looked so miserable. It wasn't how he hoped their first meeting would be.

"Yes. And Trace too. And this whole situation. All the meddling, I think I've had enough. It's not 1917 and I'm not a loveable spinster that they're trying to marry off." December answered, gloomily.

"I'm glad they interfered. I got to meet you." Tom said sweetly, trying to focus on the positive. His kind eyes warmed the very cockles of her stubborn heart and December lit up like a 1000 watt light bulb.

"Me too." she replied without hesitation. And just like that, her mood lifted. She realized she wasn't whining to just any guy. This was the man of her dreams. So she stood up straighter and poked her chest out a bit in what she hoped was an appealing way.

"You have a beautiful home. It's huge." Tom turned away to hide his grin at her, not at all subtle, mood shift.

"Thank you, I had it gut renovated from four, three bedroom apartments. I own the whole floor. So I don't plan on moving, ever." She said, glowing with pleasure. Her home was her labor of love. It was a painstakingly long process but worth it.

"I wouldn't either. I think I have a crush on your place, to be quite honest." Tom replied wistfully, making December laugh.

"Well if you're willing to leave the foyer, I can give you a quick tour?"

"I'd love that, Miss Brown."

When they finally sat down in the living room, December repeated her offer of a drink.

"What's that Manischewitz wine, you were talking about before? I'd like to try that."

"Oh! Um you don't want that. I'm sure I have a Cabernet or Burgundy somewhere that would suit your taste better." she said, blushing furiously.

"Are you ashamed of your wine of choice?" Tom joked.

"A little. All the wine drinkers I know are so snobby about what's a good wine or not. Yet when I taste it, it's awful but you can't admit that without seeming like a novice or whatever. So I keep my deliciously sweet and extremely affordable wines to myself."

"I like sweet wines." Tom tried again giving her an imploring, smoldering look. December tried not to look too giddy in response.

"No you do not. Anyone who has ever read a bio on you or heard you speak can tell that you are a total connoisseur." She scolded playfully.

"Perhaps. Okay it's true but it's not my fault. Blame my mother." He raised his hands in surrender.

"How about cappuccino instead? We can both save face that way." She offered.

"Deal. But someday you'll share it with me. I promise you that." Tom said, staring intensely at her.

"Maybe." December said, dismissing his words and his stare down as she wandered into the kitchen with him trailing behind her.

"Were you serious about not really listening to the radio?"

"And watching music television. I'm not saying I can't appreciate a good song, I'm just picky about what I listen to."

"Uh huh, so what do you like to listen to then?"

Tom sat on a tall, swiveling stool in front of the long counter, which served as her kitchen table, watching December get out milk and ingredients from the cabinets.

"Classic rock."

"You like classic rock?" she asked in disbelief.

"Yes I love it. Why?" he wondered, warily

"You just don't seem like the type that would listen to classic rock solely."

"Really? So tell me then, what do I look like I'd listen to?

"Opera." The look of shocked outrage he gave had her snorting with laughter.

"I'm sorry, but you should see your face... "She giggled helplessly.

Tom scowled at her. "Now she's insulting my face."

"No, no, you know what I mean." December stammered to explain until she caught sight of the amused expression on his face.

"I'm going to get you back for those comments, Missy" He threatened, grinning.

"So since I haven't read your Wikipedia page as yet, tell me about yourself, December Brown."

"Me? Um, what do you want to know?" she asked, uncertainly.

"Let's start with something simple, shall we? When did you know that you wanted to be a singer? As a profession, I mean."

"Hmm, well that's a hard one. Do you want the official press version or the real much less inspiring version?" December said while searching in the utensil drawer for spoons.

"The real one, of course."

"Prepare to be disappointed then..." she sighed, dramatically. Tom leaned forward with his elbows on the counter and rested his chin in the cup of his hands, the very picture of an eager listener.

"It was all Clarissa's idea. She heard me singing to myself in the girls' bathroom, that's where it all started. Prior to that we knew of each other but we didn't know each other. I just fluttered from group to group since I made friends easily. But Clarissa, even at fourteen years old, she had minions. She was always so take charge and sure of herself. Anyway, I was minding my own business singing along to whatever was playing in my CD player. She listened for a while away, then promptly yanked my headphones out of my ear and told me I was awesome. At first, I wanted to punch her in the eye but then we started talking and became fast friends. I told her how much I loved to sing because it made people happy, since I mainly sang at nursing homes and hospitals. You should have seen her face, Tom. It was hilarious. You'd have thought I told her that I was a Martian princess. Equal parts delighted and disbelieving. Anyway she said 'Wouldn't you like to be rich and famous one day? Selling out tours all over the world?' I said 'Not really, I want to be a social worker. I want to help people.' She said I could do both, that together we were going to help me make more people than I could ever know happy, just by singing. I, of course, loved the sound of that, but I didn't want to be famous. Not really, anyway. And she said and I quote 'Not to worry. That would be her job.' And so said, so done by the time we were twenty-five, Clarissa worked miracles and here I am." December finished with a flourish.

"Wow. I can't wait to meet her. She sounds like a force to be reckoned with."

"Yup. She's so focused, and detail-oriented. I sometimes wish I could be more like her. Strong, you know? Like Wonder Woman. But then I remember she's super controlling and has an aversion to taking vacations, since the world tends to fall apart without her. It's so not worth it." She said, dismissively.

Tom laughed. "I feel the same way. Just getting away from it all, I couldn't give that up."

"So, come on. It's your turn. Why did you become an actor?"

"Honestly? Telling someone else's story, just getting it out there, it really spoke to me. I tried so many other things hoping I would find my calling. Sports, politics, business. You name it; I tried it, while in university. I was decent in all of them but I couldn't see myself doing that on a day to day basis. Then one day, I saw an audition flier for a community theatre group's version of "Miss Saigon" , and I loved it. From learning the lines, to nurturing the chemistry between two characters. Everything. I love doing plays, but cinema...it's brilliant. I've never thought twice about doing anything else since the day I got my first role."

"Did you know that your whole face just lit up while you were talking? You look so happy right now." December said, smiling adoringly at him. The tips of Tom's ears reddened at her words.

"Let's move on to question two."

"Subtle change of conversation. But go ahead and ask." She quipped, while starting up the cappuccino maker to brew.

"Alright, do you have any siblings?"

"No. Do you?"

"No, but I've always wanted brothers and sisters."

"Oh, your parents didn't want any more children?" She asked, politely.

"My mother barely wanted me. Let alone ruin her body with more little hellions. Those are her words, by the way." Tom's tone was light but his words were weighted.

"I'm sure she didn't mean it like that. Tell me about your childhood? I'm a very good listener." She urged, sensing he wanted to talk.

"I thought I was supposed to be learning about you?"

"You will. Ask me anything afterward. But you go first."

"Well Alright. I've never told anyone else this before..."

"Don't worry. I promise I won't tell anyone else." She said with a conspiring wink.

He smiled gratefully at her and sighed deeply.

"My childhood consisted of being raised by various au pairs until I was five. From there I was sent to boarding school until sixteen. During which my mother moved to America and remarried four times... most of the time, I only met her husbands at the weddings, which thankfully she invited me to."

"Ouch. So I guess you two aren't very close?" December said gently, setting out two matching cup and saucers. Tom couldn't believe he was telling her all of this already but she was just so easy to talk to. Everything about her radiated warmth and understanding.

"I saw her twice a year for school holidays, where she'd take me to our husband-hunting mother-son bonding lunch date. Could you really get that close in that sort of situation?"

"Husband hunting? Were you the lure?"

"More of a scout, really. To this day, whenever I enter a restaurant I scan the room for wedding bands, and suitable suitors. It's actually very embarrassing. Checking out older men as marriage prospects...sort of makes business meetings quite awkward." Tom explained, smirking.

December guffawed at the thought of Tom in a situation like that.

"I know tons of people who would love for you to train them in the art of husband catching. In fact, Clarissa would probably drag you out clubbing, if she ever found out."

"Damn, she has my phone number. I may have to change it now." He joked.

"It's probably for the best." she said, grinning at him. "Anyway, back to your mom. How's your relationship with her now? You're both adults, so it has to be better right?"

"Actually, yes. She's been married to number four for nearly a decade, and it's the happiest I've ever seen her. You know, at Christmas time, anyway." Tom answered, with just enough bitterness to make December reach out to him. She grasped his hand and squeezed gently.

"I'm sorry. It's her loss, not yours." she said this with so much confidence it was clear that this was a personal mantra of hers.

"December?" Tom said as he threaded his fingers through hers.

"Yes?" She replied distractedly, enjoying the feel of her hands in his larger ones.

"How did you get your name?"

Chapter Ten

He felt her tense up slightly, but she didn't attempt to pull her hand away. Tom had seen last night's interview for Celebrity News. When he'd heard about her being in an orphanage for ten years, his heart went out to her. He hadn't meant to ask her such a loaded question so early on in their meeting but he couldn't shake it off of his mind.

"I was a few days old when a nun named Sister Florence found me in the park. According to her, it was the coldest December she could remember, but for some reason she wanted to go out for a walk which was unusual for her, since she isn't very outdoorsy. She said I was all bundled up in an ugly Christmas sweater. She didn't know how long I'd been out there, but there was no one else in sight."

With a faraway look in her eyes, she recited the story as if it was someone else's. Then suddenly she shrugged, like a duck shaking water off its back, this time forcing herself to connect with her origin tale. December wasn't ashamed of her orphan roots, but she really didn't relish the look of pity she received once she told someone.

"So anyway, when the officials came to take me to the orphanage they asked if she knew my name. And right at that moment, she said my eyes opened and looked at her and it was the warmest brown she'd ever seen. So when they asked her again she said December Brown. Obviously my eyes lightened up as I got older but I'm glad it didn't do it then since December Hazel sounds like a terrible eighty's hair band." She babbled with false casualness. She glanced at Tom once she was done. Ah, there it was! The pity.

"I don't know what to say." he said truthfully, rubbing soothing circles on the back of her hand with his thumb.

"I had a pretty good childhood, Tom. Sister Florence visited me each weekend with a new something she'd sewn or knitted for me. And the Children's Home wasn't so bad. I was safe and always had a hot meal and clean sheets. Not to mention the family that we made for ourselves. When I turned eleven, though, I was too old to adopt, so I was made a ward of the state. That wasn't as good. But still, I had Sister Florence and my friends. So there you have it, my sad tale that could have been worse really, so I count myself lucky." December explained, defending her tattered beginnings.

Tom leaned over and brushed his lips against her cheek in the barest of kisses but it warmed her all the way to the tips of her toes. He didn't know why he just did that, but he it felt like it was the only thing to do after hearing her admission. He wasn't sorry he asked he only wished it hadn't had to happen.

"Tom Elmswood! Are you trying to seduce me while I'm at my most vulnerable?" December asked, coyly.

"Did it work? Because that was the extent of my A-game." He said with a wiggle of his eyebrows.

"Maybe a smidge." she muttered bashfully. He was flirting with her. The sexiest man in the universe was flirting with her, in her kitchen. Best Day Ever.

"Oh, I nearly forgot. I brought éclairs." Tom strode out of the kitchen back into the living room before returning with a crumpled looking white paper bag out of his pocket. "And only slightly squished."

"It's even better when its squished." she said after he handed it to her. She practically ripped it open in excitement. December was a sucker for anything made with flour and sugar.

She moaned in delight as she sunk her teeth into the sweet pastry. Tom stared at her mouth, smirking, as she licked the chocolate glaze off of her lips.

"What are you smirking at?"

"If I knew you'd be so easy to make happy, I'd have brought you more baked goods." He responded cheekily, taking a large bit of his.

"Yup. You should have. I love pastries. Thank you. Did Clarissa tell you to bring these?" she asked, licking the creamy topping off her finger.

"No. I just thought we'd be having coffee together, why not a little sweet?" he said with a shrug. December swooned. He was utterly perfect for her. He brought dessert without being told. "Why are you looking at me like that?"

"Oh, nothing. Sorry. Just, you know, Thanks again. It was very nice of you." she tried desperately to regain her foothold in reality, and not nosedive into her usual fantasy world where Tom would kiss her senseless and then she'd don an elaborate white dress and doves would cry. She was only kidding herself, really. He was only here for damage control. Nothing more.

"It was nothing. I just really wanted to get to talk to you face to face."

"Oh." She was stunned. This was surreal and very much like the start of Tom Elmswood Fantasy number four.

"I didn't want you thinking that all I care about is my image. Because it's not true. I want to get to know you without all that extra stuff."

"Extra stuff being the paparazzi everywhere and the constant rumor mill that's publicized worldwide?"

"Precisely"

"How very gallant of you, Thomas."

"I've been told that's one of my finer points, Mademoiselle." He reached out and tapped the tip of her nose, grinning.

"Can I ask you another question?" She started cleaning up the crumbs on the kitchen counter.

"Of course. You can ask me anything." His sincerity made her look up at him, astonished. It finally hit her that he was actually serious.

"Alright, so you've mentioned your mother. What about your father?"

"I never knew him. He died not long after I was born. Unsurprisingly, since he was nearly seventy when my mother married him. He owned a chain of businesses across the England, which my mother sold after he died. It paid for my privileged upbringing and her ostentatious lifestyle."

December was speechless. Tom looked worried. Maybe he'd overloaded her too much with his cynical outlook on his family life.

94

"Let's change the subject now, before we both start crying." She finally said.

"Agreed. So what's your favorite movie?" He asked, taking a sip of the hot beverage.

"Okay now we're talking. I have a top ten list." She answered, cheerfully.

Chapter Eleven

Tom woke the next day with a smile on his face. He'd spent the entire evening at December's apartment, leaving well after ten at night. They'd talked and laughed and watched really terrible reality TV that December knew way too much about. It was the most fun he'd had in a long time. He couldn't wait to see her again. He checked his clock and saw that it was nearly 9 am. That would be too early to visit her, right? Maybe she'd be free for lunch. He'd call then, Tom thought to himself. By noon, however, he'd flagged down a cab and headed over to her place. The same doorman from the day before was on duty. He gave Tom a knowing look as he watched him hustle into the lobby.

"She's not here. Today is the fifteenth."

"What do you mean the fifteenth? Does something special happen on that day?" Tom felt bereft. He wanted to see her face so badly. He didn't even want to call just in case she said she was busy, and now apparently she was.

"The fifteenth of every month she does her incognito charity work. I'm not supposed to tell anyone but she tells me because she doesn't want people to worry. Just in case she gets kidnapped and sold on the black market. That kid watches too much crime TV." The stocky uniformed man shook his head, chuckling as he remembered her words.

"Do you know where she went exactly?"

"Well let's see, she goes to the shelter on 96th Street in the morning. Then to a nursing home in Queens around lunchtime." He checked his watch. "You might catch her there actually."

"Do you know the address?" Tom asked excitedly.

"You're lucky I saw that Trace Randall show the other day or else I wouldn't tell you Dada. She likes you, so I like you. And man, I can already tell you're hooked. She's a nice girl, so treat her right." he lectured as he wrote the address down on yellow notepad paper.

"I promise. Thank you so much." Tom said rushing out of the door, clutching the paper tightly in his hand. Where the hell is Flushing Meadows? He thought as he hopped into another taxi.

December finished placing a fresh tray of sandwiches down on the long table in the communal room of the Sunny Memories Retirement Home. Music poured through the speakers and residents either milled or danced around as their monthly party was in full swing. Damn these people can eat, December thought. She watched Mrs. Goldstein scarf down three tuna sandwiches in a matter of seconds. She'd be back in the kitchen making more food in no time, if they kept up this pace.

"Dee, they're playing my song. Come dance with me." a short, bald wrinkled man called to her. She wiped her hands on her knee length floral dress. She needed to get a grip. Mr. Bombace was nearly ninety. Yet her stupid palms were sweating. She blamed Tom for this. He had her all in a tizzy since his surprise coffee visit. He was just so sweet and easy to talk to. December struggled all morning not to call him. The media already thought she was desperate; there was no need for her to prove them right. So she busied herself by sticking to her schedule. She brought her usual bagel breakfast to the shelter she visited each month. Chatting away with the residents and helping assist in any volunteer work that was needed definitely kept her busy.

She loved her incognito outings. The people she visited didn't know or care that she was a chart topping songstress. They just knew her as Dee, the girl who came by and tried to help out as best she could. They didn't know that she donated huge chunks of money each month to help ease the burdens that non-profit organizations always bear in its never ending financial worries, even as they strive to make things better for the less fortunate.

Her favorite by far though, was the nursing home. She adored the people who lived there, as well as the staff, who knew who she was but swore to keep her secret. Retirement homes always reminded her of Sister Florence, who was the mother she wished she had. They very rarely went to the zoo or to the park when she was growing up, but December never minded much since the nun always took her on her weekly jaunts to the old folks' homes. December was spoiled rotten with cuddles, soggy kisses, and cheek pinches. And the hard candy squirreled away into her hands, away from prying eyes, weren't so bad either. For a girl who would never know her real grandparents, she had dozens over the years, that weren't related to her at all by blood or marriage but adored her nonetheless. So no matter where she lived, December always found at least one senior center to volunteer in.

Nat King Cole's dulcet tones wafted through the speakers when Mr. Bombace led her to dance floor. They swayed along to the music while she sang quietly along. It was one of Sister Florence's favorites, so she knew all the words.

"You should be a singer, DeeDee. You have such a pretty voice." Mr. Bombace mused in an admiring tone. She stifled a chuckle.

"Aw that's so sweet of you to say. You're a fantastic dancer. Is this how you won your wife over?" He nodded enthusiastically and launched into the well-known story of how they met fifty years ago.

When the music changed to a faster tempo, she barely had the chance to thank him, before being shouted for by the nursing home grumpy pants, Mr. Reese. The tall, gaunt man was argumentative and rude except on party days when he was only demanding. December hurried over to dance with him; unfortunately, it was to a song she wasn't entirely sure about.

"I don't know if I know the steps to this one."

"Just follow my lead, little Miss." he twirled her around, suddenly causing her to squeak in surprise. "Get ready for a dip."

Her eyes bulged at his words. The last time he'd tried that, she'd fallen flat on the floor.

"May I cut in?"

Oh thank God, she thought. It didn't matter who it was just as long as she didn't have to suffer another bruised back. She looked over at her savior and gasped. There stood the man of her dreams looking just as sexy in jeans and a red cable knit sweater as he did in a suit.

"Tom? What are you doing here?"

He opened his mouth to answer but the elderly man between them interrupted.

"DeeDee, you didn't tell me you had a boyfriend." Mr. Reese scowled in Tom's general direction.

"Oh, he's just a friend. You don't have to be jealous." December said with a wink.

"Well, you should tell him that. 'Cause he's got that look in his eye." He grumbled, shuffling over to the quickly emptying food table. When Tom took her hand to dance, she hesitantly wrapped her arms around his neck when she felt his hands encircle her waist.

"What are you doing here?" She repeated, even though she was overjoyed to see him.

"The doorman at your place told me where to find you. I wanted to see you again." He admitted.

"Damn that Martin! I told him to keep that quiet unless the cops came around asking questions." she muttered. Tom smiled as he studied her face.

"You look wonderful." He whispered into her ear. And she did. She kept looking more radiant each time he saw her.

"So do you." She whispered back, her face tingling with the blush to end all blushes. How was she supposed to be cool and collected when he kept saying sweet things like that to her.

"Um, Tom, about the just friends' thing…"

"I understand."

"You do?"

"Yes. I'll have to sweep you off your feet before that scary older gentleman does."

101

December laughed. "Yeah, that sounds about right."

They finished the dance in a comfortable silence, swaying gently to the slow song. Afterwards, December led them over to the refreshments table.

"So what is this party celebrating?" Tom asked as he sipped his awful, room temperature, sugar free fruit punch.

"S.S. Day." Mrs. Johnson piped in.

"Is that a German thing?" Tom questioned, politely.

"See I told you it would sound like something to do with World War II." December said triumphantly. The curly haired elderly woman waved off her concerns with a "Bah" .

"It's not German. It's Social Security Day." She explained as she led them over to a quieter spot.

"So they're celebrating getting their pension checks?" He was a little confused on how that would be cause for a party.

"Not exactly. It's just a reason to have a party because everyone wanted sheet cake and they're only allowed it on festive occasions."

Tom raised an eyebrow. "Is it really good sheet cake?"

"Uh...let's not get too overly critical about this." She answered, cagily. He snorted into his drink.

"So Tom Elmswood, what do you do for fun? Hang out with friends? Clubbing? Parcheesi tournaments?" December speculated while eyeing up the pile of cheese puffs.

Tom was stumped. He was used to this question in his profession but he knew that his usual line about traveling would feel fraudulent like it always did. This time however, he wanted to tell December the truth, that he lived a solitary life.

In his quest to avoid the emotional void the lack of relationship with his parents left, he'd also avoided building close bonds with people. Tom, like December lived a sheltered life, except his wasn't a cocoon carefully constructed by people who loved him and wanted to preserve his goodness in a sometimes cruel, harsh world. His was of his own making. His good looks made his reserved personality seem charming and debonair as opposed to aloof and standoffish. Though he never had a problem making friends, he hadn't had a best friend since he was nine. Not even a group of boisterous buddies that blew into town once a year. Even in school, he'd flitted through social groups, being cool enough not to be bullied, but not so much that he got invited to parties. Out of sight and out of mind was his unofficial stance on relationships in general. And up till now he'd never felt like he was missing anything.

Now here he was yearning for an emotional connection to this wonderful woman whom he'd only met days ago.

"I'm quite good at tennis but mostly I read a lot." he finally said, feeling ashamed at his paltry offering.

"Really? Me too. What's your favorite genre?" December asked brightly.

"I read nonfiction. Mostly biographies." He winced at his boring admission.

"Tom, are you OK? Do you have a tummy ache? Was it the tuna sandwiches?" she asked worriedly. He looked a little off.

"I'm fine. I'm just feeling a little self-conscious. I'm not very interesting." He turned away from her, not wanting to see the look on her face.

December slid her arms around his waist, startling him from his sulk. He instinctively pulled her closer, marveling at how wonderful she felt in his arms. She rested her head against his chest.

"I read menus. That's my favorite genre even though I tell people its fiction. But yeah, I collect restaurant menus so I could spend like an hour pouring over them. See? No need to feel embarrassed because I won this round. By the way, please don't tell anyone I do that."

Tom chuckled at her confession, feeling touched that she shared her secret with him. He rested his chin on her head enjoying the feel of curvy body against his.

"You're secret is safe with me."

"Good." she mumbled.

"Your hair smells fantastic."

December's heart raced at his words. Not even in her daydreams did Fantasy-Tom ever say something like that to her. Then again, she hadn't anticipated having him here with her in Flushing, Queens in the first place.

"You smell really good too." she whispered, bravely. Tom's grin couldn't have been wider if he tried.

"Hey love birds, get a room already." Mrs. Johnson broke in, shooing them apart.

Chapter Twelve

Later, after they'd cleaned up the remains of the party, Tom helped December into her coat.

"Thank you for all your help today. It was really nice to have some company."

"It was fun. I've never done anything like this before but I could get used to it." Tom hadn't known what to expect from today, only that he wanted to be where she was.

As luck would have it, he was pleasantly surprised. He'd never had any cause to be around the elderly, so it was all new to him. He wasn't enamored by the romantic aspect of it like December clearly was, but he was fascinated by the different ways the seniors coped with this way of life. There was definitely a deep sense of loss and sadness permeating, yet they still made their own community.

"Really? That would be so amazing, Tom!"

"Do you have any more plans for today?"

"No I was going to head home. You?" she tried to keep the eagerness out of her voice.

"I'm all yours for the day." He said taking her hand as they walked outside. "Is it odd that this is my first time walking around in Queens?"

"It's not as surprising as you think. Lots of Manhattanites just pass through to get to JFK airport. But it's great here because most of the time nobody even bothers to look at you let alone mob you for an autograph. I do all my Christmas shopping here too. It's nice being anonymous sometimes, you know?"

"Do you think I could do that too?" Tom asked sounding genuinely excited at the idea.

"Of course you can. During the holidays it's all so hectic that nobody gives a damn about who you are as long as you don't cut in line." She explained, warming at the thought of taking him around Queens without being hassled by the paparazzi, who liked to pretend a huge borough didn't exist.

"Do you want to see a movie?"

"Like at the cinema?"

"Yes. There's a movie theatre not too far away from here. It's really small and the guy at the concession stand has a really bad attitude but..."

"I would love to."

"Really?"

"Yes. Oh god I feel like such a tourist but I would love to. I haven't been in an actual cinema in years."

"Well geez, I would have offered earlier if I'd known. Come on I'm parked over there." She said pointing to a small blue Volvo. It wasn't the most exciting of cars but it was all the better to blend in with. No one looked twice at you when you drove an obviously used car.

"You drive?"

"You get surprised a lot, don't you?" December said, shooting him an amused look.

"Apparently. I can't imagine Clarissa would let you drive all the way here by yourself."

"Clarissa isn't my boss, Tom. Well that's not entirely true. She's very bossy. But she's my best friend first. I'm my own person."

"I didn't mean to offend you. It's just that I'm once again a bit envious. I've been trapped by a rigid set of rules since childhood because I was born into a wealthy household. And you know more than anyone else how restrictive life is for you once you're famous. So yes, I know how to drive, solely because it's a rite of passage. But I haven't had much of a chance to actually drive since I've always had a personal driver or used taxis."

"Would you like to drive today, Tom?" December offered, holding out her car keys.

"Do you mean it?" he said even as he took them from her.

Chapter Thirteen

Twenty minutes and one hair-raising drive later, they'd finally arrived at the theatre.

"God that felt good!" Tom crowed proudly.

"Err yes. Maybe you should get more practice?" December un-gripped the seat belt she'd been holding onto for dear life while Tom nearly careened them into endless oncoming and sometimes stationary vehicles.

"Oh I'm so sorry, sweetheart. Was it that bad?" He stroked his hand through her silky dark hair causing her eyes to flutter close at his touch. December didn't trust herself to speak so she shook her head and pretended she didn't melt into a puddle when he called her sweetheart. The car ride from hell was worth it just for the term of endearment alone.

"You look beautiful even when you're lying by omission. Did you know that?" Tom tucked a stray strand behind her ear and hopped out of the car. He'd opened her door by the time she'd stopped trembling enough to unhook her seat belt.

"Shall we call this our first date?" he continued, nonchalantly. He entwined their fingers together, pulling her along.

"December?" he tried again, she hadn't said a word since the car. And he was starting to get worried. She shook herself from her frozen state, mumbling something about the bathroom and ran off, leaving Tom confused in the lobby of the movie theatre.

December closed the door to the bathroom stall and leaned against it. She was in shock. He wanted this to be a date. How in the world had this happened? She phoned Clarissa barely even looking at the screen.

"Hey Dee, what's up?"

"Tom. Date. Flushing."

"What? I need full sentences, girl. Breathe deep and repeat."

"Tom wants this to be our first date. We're at the movies in Flushing." she spat out after a few sputtering tries.

"Ooh so you're panicking in the restroom now right?"

"Yes! My heart won't stop racing and he called me sweetheart and said I looked beautiful and what do I do, Clarissa? Do I run?"

"Why would you run? No! Focus! This is Tom Elmswood. The guy whose movies you made me watch a billion times just so you could memorize his face, remember?"

December nodded even though Clarissa couldn't see her through the phone

"And you swore to me you'd marry him if he even looked your way just once, remember that?"

"I'm not entirely sure I said that second part."

"Good you've got your voice back. And yes you did. You said you would marry him and adopt eight kids and name one of them Mr. Roboto."

"Oh yeah I did say that."

"Uh huh. Now go out there and get your guy. 'Cause I want to be an auntie by the time I'm thirty-two."

"Wait a minute. Why aren't you surprised that I'm in Queens? "

"GPS tracking. The surveillance team alerts me whenever you leave Manhattan. Toodles." she hung up before December could tell her off.

Tom's face lit up seeing her exit the ladies room. Concern lined his face as he walked up to her. It was a little hard to breathe with him standing so close.

"Are you alright, December?" He asked. She nodded, not trusting her throat to not embarrass her with a croak or something just as ghastly.

"Are you sure?" he caressed her cheek with the back of his hand, his eyes a smoldering ocean blue searching her hazel ones.

"I'm fine now. I just, um, I just needed a minute but I'm okay now." she admitted, feeling a little foolish that she made him worry over nothing.

Tom breathed a sigh of relief, pulling her into a hug. "I'm glad you didn't run off screaming through the streets."

111

December was very glad that he couldn't see the look on her face at how close to the truth he was. She simply snuggled deeper into the embrace.

"I like you, December Brown. Probably more than I've ever like anyone else in my whole life. And I know you don't believe me as yet but I promise I'll prove it to you."

She decided to take the bait and whispered, "How?"

"Well first, we're going to see a terribly cheesy horror movie that I've already bought the tickets for, and I'm going to hold your hand the entire time. And since this is our first date, I'm going to spring for popcorn. Extra butter."

"What about a soda?"

"Anything you like." He assured.

"A hot dog, maybe?"

"Definitely not" She swatted his arm playfully, returning his impish grin.

After the movie, which was as bad as advertised, December drove them to a long term parking lot, just outside of the city. After explaining to Tom that her driver will pick them up in a few minutes, they settled down to wait.

"Do you want to go back to my place? Get your mind out of the gutter, Missy. I just want to show you my apartment. Maybe have some dinner later?" he smirked.

He loved watching her face. How she tried and miserably failed to stop her emotions from flashing plain as day with every adorable thought that passed through her pretty head. She must have been awful at poker since he could already read her face like a book. Like how the look on her face just now, told him how carefully he should tread with her.

"Oh, well then, I'd love to." She said relief washing over her features.

December felt like she was sixteen again and all the awkward excitement that came with it. It wasn't like she hadn't had boyfriends before. In fact, in high school, she'd made out with more than her fair share. She and Clarissa weren't very picky when it came to locking lips with the opposite sex back in those days. But sometime around her first album after a long slew of kissing and fondling models in her music videos, her dating inclination dried up. Boys she could handle, men not so much. Maybe she was waiting for Mr. Right or maybe she was just scared. Either way, she'd never had a serious boyfriend. And now here she was getting close to the man of her dreams and she was torn between wanting to hide under her blankets in bed, and kiss him senseless.

"What's your favorite kind of food?"

"What? Oh sorry, I love Polish food. Well anything Eastern European to be honest."

"Really? That's odd. I was really hoping you'd say something I could easily make."

"It's not odd. It's yummy. You cook?" She looked both mystified and intrigued. Tom couldn't decide if that was exactly a good thing.

"Yes. I learned shortly after University. Do you?"

"Sometimes. My housekeeper usually does it though. Malina always leaves enough for leftovers. That's where I got my love for Polish cuisine."

"Oh that explains it then. Does she live with you?"

"People still do that? No, but she comes in three days a week to make sure I'm not living in a pile of filth, eating out of the garbage." She remarked, rummaging through her handbag, for her phone. No matter how careful she was her phone seemed to sink straight to the bottom of her handbag. Just like her keys.

"You say the cutest things." December shot him an incredulous glance. "Don't give me that look, it's true. I never know what you're going to say next. It's very thrilling."

"It's not nice to poke fun at people, Sir"

"I'm not. I mean it. Can I tell you a secret?" he murmured, conspiratorially

"Sure?"

"I don't have many friends."

December's heart broke at his confession. She didn't know how she'd survive without her friends. They were the only real family she had. And knowing about Tom's childhood only made the whole affair sadder. She grabbed his hand, clutching it close to her heart, as if she was swearing an oath to him.

"I'll be your friend. You can share my friends too if you like. In fact, you can have Trace." She desperately wanted to wipe away the sadness lodged deeply in his eyes. He smiled a crooked smile and gazed adoringly at her.

He'd never been this open with anyone before but with December, he couldn't help himself. He wanted to know everything about her. He wanted her to know everything about him. And more than anything else, he wanted to know that she accepted him just as he was. With no airs and graces. No fancy suits and polished lines, just Tom. Slightly lonely, starved for affection, Tom.

Although he acted in his fair share of romantic films, and had enough girlfriends in his past to remind him that he was a red blooded male, he very rarely sought people to embrace. To be quite honest, he couldn't name anyone off the top of his head, that he was overly fond of. Maurice, maybe? Not really. Theirs was a business relationship. Patrick? Definitely not. He would ditch him the second his star began to wane. His mother? She of the air kisses and frosty demeanor? If his university graduation taught him anything, it was that his mother did not feel that hugging him was part of her obligation as his only living parent. Even his own housekeeping staff merely tolerated him, as he did them.

Tom gently pulled their joined hands towards closer and softly kissed December's knuckles. No, Tom hadn't had much practice in being a real boy so he grew up into a somewhat wooden man. But something about the honey-hued brunette beside him made him feel real for the first time. He couldn't stop himself from touching her as much as possible as if somehow her inner sunshine spread to him, making him alive and tangible. He didn't bother to hide his feelings from her because he'd been hidden too long already. Two days of knowing her and he felt like he'd found himself again. There was no way he could go back to his shell of a life without her. If she'd have him, that is.

Tom stood up suddenly, taking December with him. She looked bewildered since he seemed lost in his thoughts and hadn't responded to her offer of friendship.

"Tom, are you okay?" she asked, guardedly. What if he'd changed his mind and would rather be alone than be friends with her and her family? Upon hearing her voice, he moved to stand in front of her, looking into beseechingly into her eyes.

"Do you still have a crush on me, December?" he held her gaze. She sputtered in in surprise.

115

Tom bit his lip feeling slightly ashamed of himself for blurting out something like that but only slightly. For some crazy reason he desperately wanted to hear her admit it. Her breathy, whispered answer surged through him like an adrenaline high.

"That's a relief because I have such a crush on you, Miss Brown." He leaned in smiling.

Tilting her face towards his, he softly kissed her parted lips. December tasted sweet from something uniquely her and oh so warm. Tom had only meant to kiss her once but after the first one, he swept in for a second deeper kiss. She responded instinctively the first time. And when the next kiss came, she drank him in as much as he did her, wrapping her arms around his neck. Hungrily, their canoodling continued until they both were forced to stop for air.

"So who's your favorite singer?" Tom inquired, randomly, while tracing his thumb lightly across her bottom lip. There was no way she was concentrating especially since her eyes were glazed over with bliss.

"Huh?"

"Singer. Name your favorite."

"Oh I can't say, especially since you're at a disadvantage already with your lack of musical knowledge. It just wouldn't be fair." She said in a saccharine sweet but plenty sly way.

"Oh you naughty girl." Tom tickled her shamelessly, reveling in her exuberant shrieking.

Chapter Fourteen

"You don't play fair." December gasped, stifling another moan as he kissed her senseless against his apartment door. "How am I supposed to know where you live if you keep distracting me?"

"I'll give you my address." Tom murmured, huskily against her mouth.

She was a fantastic kisser and he just couldn't get enough of her lips. Only the ding of the hallway elevator forced them apart and he finally unlocked the door they'd been leaning against for the better part of ten minutes.

"Welcome to my humble abode, Ms. Brown." he pushed open the door wider and ushered her in. His condominium was chic and modern in its décor, and more than a little cold. In all its sleekness and stark detail, it looked like something out of a model home magazine.

"Wow!" December said in amazement. "It's so big and classy!" She tried very hard to look for more adjectives to describe the cavernous penthouse, but it was very hard. If he'd actually decorated it himself, she'd buy a hat just to eat it.

"I know it barely looks lived in. It came furnished, so I didn't have to bother." He explained at her slightly bemused expression, which quickly changed to one of complete understanding.

"I guessed as much..." she mused as she continued to look around in wonder. Wall to wall ceiling to floor windows exposed a breath-taking view of the city. It was gorgeous to look at, but not enough to want to live in this empty, heartless place.

Tom deserved something more. Something filled with all the warmth and sweetness he exuded without knowing it. Or at least a comfy couch. Would it hurt to have something that looked like you could fall asleep on it? He scratched the back of his neck looking a little out of sorts.

"Maybe I could get a rug?" he offered helpfully. Or was it helplessly? December gave him a mischievous grin that he couldn't help returning.

"What's that smile about, young lady?"

"You should get a bear skin rug." she declared, feigning seriousness.

"Oh dear." he said, reproachfully. She nodded as if he'd agreed before continuing her decorating scheme.

"And shag carpeting. Ooh and a water bed." December dissolved into giggles as Tom swept her into a bear hug and nibbled her neck. Her cell phone began vibrating and ringing in her still worn coat pocket, startling them both.

"Sorry, I need to take this." she said scowling at the caller's name.

"Of course. I'll go start dinner since you refused my buttery popcorn offer." He kissed the tip of her nose, helped her take off her coat finally and wandered away.

December watched him walk in to the kitchen, letting the caller try again. It was Trace finally crawling back and she didn't think he deserved a quick response. Let him stew for a little longer. She wasn't mad at him anymore, since his cockeyed matchmaking attempt panned out in the end. Tom freaking kissed her. Like a lot. So yeah, she wasn't mad at him about that anymore, but he betrayed her trust and privacy. Though many people confused her innate kindness for weakness, December Brown wasn't a complete pushover.

Trace's name popped up on her screen again. This time she picked up.

"Yes?"

"Hi Dee, it's me. Can we talk?" he asked sounding extremely sheepish. Good. No mercy.

"Fine." She kept her voice cold and flat. It wasn't an easy feat since she was so gloriously happy she wanted to share it with what had to be their number one supporter. Instead she allowed him to ramble and babble and squirm.

"Listen, I'm so sorry about everything. I betrayed every friendship code by showing that text on my show. I should have warned you at the very least. But my heart was in the right place, I mean if there was ever two people who needed a little romance, it was you two. I mean, I know I shouldn't have pushed so hard but I was in cupid mode and my astrologer said..."

December couldn't stop herself from laughing. Trace and his damned astrology fixation, it was his excuse for all sorts of horrible decisions that actually sometimes worked themselves out in the end.

"You're laughing. That's good right? We're on the road to forgiveness then? Maybe?" He hedged nervously, hopeful.

"He kissed me" she whispered excitedly into the phone. Trace's shout of 'I knew it' nearly deafened her but her goofy grin only widened.

"Shh, you can't tell anyone. Or else..." she figured that suggested all kinds of gruesome things she'd do to him if he ever crossed her again.

"I absolutely promise. So is he a good kisser? You have to promise me that if you two ever get engaged, you'll announce it on my show first!"

"Calm yourself, man. We literally just met. But duh yes! Hello, pushy matchmaking cupid astrology addict whoever, you weren't wrong. And it was amaze-balls." she gushed, looking around in case Tom snuck up on her to eavesdrop on her gossip fest.

"Hold on, you're whispering. Oh my God, is he there? Are you at his place?" Trace's excitement ratcheted up his already high voice.

"Yes but he's busy making dinner. Now I have to go. I love you again so goodbye." She laughed as he shrieked over the idea of Tom making dinner.

"I love you too, honey. I'm glad you don't hate me anymore. Call me later and we'll do lunch. Kisses!" After he hung up, December took a moment to collect herself, before going in search of Tom and his kitchen.

"Was that Trace on the phone?" he asked, glancing up from where he stood, expertly chopping a zucchini into chunks.

"Yup. How'd you guess?" she said wandering over closer to him.

"Sound carries on parquet flooring..." He gave a knowing smirk.

"Oh God, you heard everything, didn't you?"

"You have a pretty loud whisper." December's eyes widened then narrowed at his comment.

"Emphasis on pretty." He backtracked, as her eyes narrowed even further to tiny slits. Undeterred, he nuzzled the crook of her neck, reveling in her light floral scent.

"I'm glad that you two made up and that I don't have to punch him at the next industry party we both attend."

"You wouldn't." she said breathily, her eyes fluttered closed when nuzzling slowly became gentle kisses on her throat.

"I would. For you, I would."

"That's so chivalrous. It's really, really nice..." she gave him a small peck, and backed away before she forgot herself. Tom winked at her, and resumed cutting up vegetables.

"Would you like to know what I'm cooking especially for you tonight?"

"Yes. Please wow me. I desperately need to know."

"Well cheeky girl, I'm making pasta primavera."

"While that sounds yummy, how is that especially for me?"

"It's all I had in the fridge. It was either that or sardines and toast."

"Ah yes. How romantic. Do you need any help?"

"No, you just have a seat and be gorgeous while I wow you with my culinary skills."

"Where'd you learn to cook?" she watched him swiftly slice tomatoes like they do on Food Network, and was indeed, suitably impressed.

"France. After university, I spent a year in culinary school there. I can bake too." he said nonchalantly. December sat open mouthed. She'd read every biography article on him, in her most stalkerish times, and never heard about his cooking prowess. Of course, she couldn't tell him that without sounding like a creep.

"Oh wow, that's so awesome." The smile he gave her was pure sunshine, warm and captivating. For a man who was exposed to so much fawning adoration daily, he seemed genuinely thrilled to hear those words from her.

Tom wiped his hands on a kitchen towel, opened his counter top wine chiller to pull out a bottle and two stemmed glasses.

"So I know you weren't ready to share your favorite wine with me as yet, so I did a little research on sweet wine, and this one came highly recommended." he poured the gold colored liquid into a glass and handed to her, waiting expectantly for her to try it.

December felt touched at his attempt. He actually looked up wines that he thought she might like. He'd failed of course, like everyone else who thought they could convert her. She liked Moscato but despised the sickeningly sweet desert wines. Still she smiled happily at Tom's eager face, while anticipating the worst. Her first sip was surprisingly pleasant, and her face showed it.

"This is lovely. What is it?" she eyed the expensive looking bottle with its French writing. It was no Manischewitz but it would do, if only to stop him from trying again.

"It's Sauternes from Chateau Suduiraut." he said in perfect pronunciation that made her flush in delight.

"Sounds pricey."

"If you like it, then it's not." He stated, casually.

"I like it. Thank you." she took another sip, he grinned happily.

Tom carried on preparing their meal in thoughtful silence, as December flipped through a magazine he had lying around.

"Do you sew?" He asked suddenly.

"Um that's a little random but yeah I can do basic patchwork sewing stuff. Why?" She answered, warily. If he thought she'd be darning his socks or whatever, he was barking up the wrong tree.

"Well you know how sometimes the needle and thread refuse to synch up and you keep snipping at the thread because you think somehow that would help?"

"Uh yea sure..."

'And how when you finally get the thread lined up just right and it goes through, you just know? Like you don't even have to be really looking for it to happen but once that tiny piece of string goes in, no one has to tell you that you've finally done it. You just know. Straight to your bones?" he probed, animatedly.

"This analogy is a little confusing but yes, I know what you mean." December replied, gently, waiting for him to continue.

"Sorry. My point is what if that's what finding your soul mate is like? That you're the needle and the threads are different people in your life but once the one for you shows up, you just know by gut instinct. And you didn't need to have your heartbroken a billion times to know it." he clarified, willing her with his eyes to understand what he was trying to say.

"I never thought of it that way but yes. That's what I always hoped finding your soul mate would be like. Like finding that missing piece of the puzzle." she said gazing just as intensely back at him.

The sizzling of the pan brought them out of their joint reverie, with averted eyes and flushed cheeks.

After dinner they sat cuddling on his uncomfortable couch. His arms wrapped around her shoulders as her head rested on his chest, listening to his heartbeat and deep breaths. She couldn't remember ever feeling so content.

"Maybe we could go for a walk in the park tomorrow?" Tom pondered aloud, breaking the easy silence. December made a face he couldn't see. It was freezing out, why would anyone want to be out there wandering, unless they really had to?

"Maybe have a mini picnic?" His ideas were getting worse. She loathed picnics in warm weather, why would she like it in a practically Arctic winter? She never understood the fascination with picnics in the first place. Didn't people know about ticks and Lyme disease? Not to mention the uncomfortable ground with ants and other creepy crawlies. Perhaps Tom wasn't as flaw free as she thought he was.

"December? What do you think?" he prodded following her lack of response.

"Sure, that sounds great." she lied through her teeth, figuring she could suffer through a bone chilling walk since it was Tom after all. "How about we go get hot chocolate afterward instead?"

"Oh that's a much better idea." He kissed her temple. "To be honest, I only suggested a picnic because that's a go to answer to a walk in the park. I don't really get that whole laying on dirt to eat a sandwich business."

"I think I love you!" December blurted out, staring up at him in adoration then shock at her own words "Um no I didn't mean that...I meant that I feel the same way about picnics? Uh Lyme disease..." she finished weakly.

Tom's eyes twinkled in delight and kissed the fingers on her right hand one by one. "It's too late, sweetheart. I know your secret already." He teased.

Chapter Fifteen

Hours later after he'd bundled her into a private car and seen her off safely, Tom reminisced about how different he felt and acted around her. December had fallen asleep, with her head on his lap as he played with her hair. He knew it was probably because they'd been watching a documentary on mountain goats that could bring anyone to tears. They hadn't really been paying too much attention to it except to snicker here and there, mostly focusing on talking about anything and everything under the sun.

Tom had never felt so content just sitting there twirling strands of her shiny brown hair through his fingers, watching her pout in her sleep. He'd never been so love struck as he'd been when her eyes' fluttered open, and she'd given him a groggy still full of sleep smile that melted his heart. He could certainly get used to that, he thought to himself as he got ready for bed. The idea of waking up to December every day put the goofiest smile on Tom's face as he snuggled down into his sheets.

The next morning as he drank his coffee, he called Maurice to check in.

"About time. Did you work everything out with her? Are you back in Clarissa Gregory's good graces?" his agent demanded, gruffly, in lieu of a hello.

"Yes I think so. We're having hot chocolate later today, after her training session. She's great, Maurice. You'd really like her."

"Uh huh" Maurice's bored sigh should have alerted Tom to the level of not really caring he had on the topic, but no. He hadn't even noticed.

"No really, she's sweet and funny. Not to mention absolutely breath-taking, especially when she laughs." Tom added dreamily.

"Yeah, well. Try not to screw it up. Anyway, I'm emailing you the flight itinerary for your upcoming trip. Everything's all booked up. Just need you to confirm. Any problems let me know." Maurice stated in his usual monotone delivery and hung up.

"I really need to get new friends." Tom said to the dial tone.

It was times like these that truly made him realize how lonely he was. Good times or bad, he didn't have anyone to talk it over with. He wanted to share his news with someone who would be happy for him. He wanted to call December but he couldn't do that, not when it was she who he wanted to discuss. He suddenly felt desperate. So much so that he very nearly called his mother.

That snapped him out of it. Then he thought about it again, and dialed her up. Maybe he was too harsh on her. Perhaps she was just trying to do her best for him, and it all got misconstrued along the way.

"Hello, Mother." Tom said nervously upon hearing her voice answer the phone.

"Thomas? Is that you?"

"Yes. How are you?" he said, warming to the idea of having a normal out of the blue conversation with her.

"Why are you calling? Do you need something?" she asked suspiciously.

"No. I just wanted to say hello." Tom regretted the whole thing. He suddenly felt deflated. And it wasn't even a minute into the call yet.

"Oh. Well it's good of you to call. I saw that show you were on the other night. Your stepfather loves Trace Randall, you know."

"Really?" he was intrigued. His mother watched television? He always assumed she lived in a sort of pocket of reality where that sort of mundane thing didn't exist. He'd envisioned her as more of a drink herself into coma nightly kind of wealthy woman.

"Yes, of course I did. I watch everything you're in." she stated nonchalantly.

"You do?" Tom was utterly shocked. He didn't think she even remembered that he was an actor. Let alone a successful one.

"What mother wouldn't be proud of having a son like you? I talk about you all the time to the girls at my knitting club."

Tom nearly pinched himself. Never in a billion years did he think he'd hear those words out of her mouth.

"Wait. You knit?"

His mother laughed. He could count on both hands how many times he'd heard her laugh. But this time was his favorite.

"No, but since you keep being shocked silly over everything I say, I thought I'd tease you a little." she said, light-heartedly.

"Sorry." he replied sheepishly.

"Thomas, about that show. I know you've gotten a lot of flak over it, but you were a gentleman through and through. You shouldn't feel ashamed at all. Although..."

"Although what?"

"She's wonderful. What are you waiting for?" She gently admonished.

"Well actually, we've been seeing each other for the past couple of days. She's even better in person." He confided, blushing even though he was all alone in his apartment.

"That's what Charles said. He's met her a few times over the years when she sung at the annual stroke awareness fundraiser that his company sponsors. Even before she became famous. He and I adore her music. I can't believe you'd never heard of her before."

"I have particular tastes." he explained, tiredly. He'd never live it down if his fifty-six year old mother and stepfather knew about December before he did.

"Yes, yes, classic rock, I remember. Still it's no excuse. I can't wait to meet her. Maybe you can bring her over for Christmas?"

"Don't you think it's a little soon to be asking her about spending the holidays together?" Tom asked. He'd make a list of all the things his mother said to him today that pleasantly surprised him. Her knowing his favorite musical genre made the Top 5 list.

"Not if she's the one. You'll know that right off the bat." His mother said sagely. Tom smiled knowingly to himself.

"I'll ask her. And I'll let you know in a few weeks' time, alright?"

"You do that, darling. Now you called me to talk about something didn't you?"

Chapter Sixteen

"It was so surreal. She even apologized for being an absentee parent. She said there was a cancer scare that made her realize how bad she'd let things become between us. How she wanted to call me then but didn't think I'd be very welcoming. She said she barely knew her own son and she wanted to try to have a real relationship with me." Tom quipped, regarding his earlier phone call as he held the door open for her.

After a very short walk in the park, where Tom realized he really didn't want to freeze to death and December pretended to be mildly disappointed, they'd stopped at a nearly empty Starbucks.

"Oh Tom! That's great news right?" She slid into the seat opposite him in the furthest corner of the franchised coffeehouse. From this angle they couldn't be seen from the windows and they would be able to see anyone approaching them. On top of the matching horn rimmed glasses for subtle disguises that December provided, Tom felt pretty secure.

"I think so. I think I'm still in shock though. My mother was always this elusive figure in my life and now she wants to be part of it. I didn't think I'd be so forgiving, you know? But everyone deserves a second chance right?"

"Yes they do. Well nearly everyone. But yes your mom certainly does."

"She said you've met my stepfather before at a fundraiser for his company about stroke awareness. He's the CEO."

"Charlie Yeats is your step dad? Wow what a small world."

"I don't think I've ever spoken more than two sentences to the man"

"You should. He's really lovely. You'd like him."

"Is he? Well my mother wanted to know if you'd like to spend Christmas with us. I know it's too soon..."

"I would love to. I mean if you want me to, that is." her face was flushed with excitement.

December alternated her Christmases between Terrence and Clarissa's broods. While they always made her feel welcomed, she didn't truly feel at home. She was just that extra place setting for the person who had nowhere else to go.

"More than anything." He grinned, tugging the tasseled pompoms that dangled from her pink knitted hat. He leaned over and kissed her lightly. "So what would you like drink?"

"Peppermint hot chocolate, grande, skim milk." she recited automatically.

"Nice. I'll be right back" He stood up and stretched, allowing his long-sleeved t-shirt to ride up. The peak of exposed skin seemed to ensnare December's focus. Tom smirked to himself; at least he wasn't the only one fawning.

December fiddled around in her bag, trying not to stare too obviously at Tom's profile. Even with the glasses or especially with the glasses, he was still hubba hubba hot. Now with sexy, nerd flair. She wouldn't have been the least bit surprised if Tom was recognized by someone in the cafe. The other customers and the staff were already straining their necks to catch a glimpse of him. With his model looks, and those soul searing pale blue eyes paired with his raven hair, he was memorable.

Meanwhile, all she had to do was put on the pink pullover hat that Marilyn had knitted her for her birthday, and she was pretty much invisible. December wasn't complaining; she liked being able to merge with the masses. Tom, however, would have to try harder with disguises. Maybe a goatee and tinted glasses might help.

Her phone rang, yanking her out of her thoughts. She smiled at the caller's name before answering.

"Hi, Nunny."

"My poor DeeDee cakes, are you okay? I just saw the TV footage. Do you need me to come visit you for a few days? I know you had your heart set on him, but he seems cold and aloof to me. Handsome he may be, but you don't need him."

"He's not cold. He's dreamy, Nunny. He's buying me hot cocoa as we speak." she whispered the last part into the phone.

"Ooh that's good right? You love chocolate. So there's no crisis, then?"

"Nope. Not at all. We've kissed a few times, too."

"Dear Lord, you're too young to date. Wait sorry, sorry, I just had a flash back to your teenage years. Don't mind me."

December giggled. "You're silly. Are you okay, Nunny? Do you need anything?"

"I'm alright, lovely girl. Why don't you bring him to my surprise party on Saturday? I need him to pass my test."

"What test?" She asked suspiciously.

"A none of your business test. Just bring him. I want to meet him. And that way he gets to meet everyone at once, right?"

"That's true. I'll invite him. Actually he's on his way back now. I'll call you later. Love you."

"Love you too, Deedles." She placed the phone down on the small wooden table just as he arrived with their orders.

Tom set down their drinks while sliding into his chair "So, I think I have a date on Friday with the guy who made our drinks."

December snickered. "Awesome. Do you think he recognized you?"

"No, I think we're fine. So I wasn't eavesdropping, but can I ask who Nunny is?" he queried, clearly intrigued. He had inkling but wanted to hear it from her.

"Sister Florence. Remember the nun who found me as an infant? Well, we never lost touch. She's the closest thing I've ever had to a mother. When I was learning to talk, I kept calling her 'Mommy'. And she kept correcting me. Telling me that she was a nun and couldn't be my mom. Long story short, I sort of morphed both words, calling her Nunny. And I've called her that ever since." She answered without hesitation, more than happy to tell him about someone she obviously adored.

"That's really sweet."

"She pretended to try to talk me out of it a couple of times, because she's married to God and the church and all. But secretly, she loves it. She's the best." She said, her eyes shining with love.

"Well I can't wait to meet her." Tom remarked enthusiastically

"That's wonderful because she wants to invite you to her birthday shindig on Saturday. If you're free and willing, that is"

"For you? Always." he said with a wink that set her off blushing.

"Really? You'll come? Don't you have something Hollywood to do on a Saturday night?" she asked stunned at his interest.

"Does surfing the web and watching reruns count as Hollywood?" he deadpanned.

"Not in the slightest." She giggled, her mind drifting to thoughts of them curled up next to each other, with their eyes glued to a laptop screen. She sighed happily.

"Then I'd love to come. Will I get to meet the rest of the gang? "He questioned eagerly

"Yay! It's nothing big or exciting just our core group of people at Nunny's favorite restaurant. We book the back room and the karaoke machine. We like to keep it low key."

"That sounds promising, I'll bring a camera." He teased.

"No way, Tom. You can't." she said laughing. "Anyway, it's only about seven of us in total."

"Alright, let me see if I remember their names correctly. And you'll fill me in on the rest, okay?"

"Sure. Go on."

"Clarissa, I'm familiar with already. She's your agent right?"

"And manager and bestest best friend in the whole wide world." December added proudly.

"Lucky you. I've been trying to befriend my manager, Maurice, for years, and I've got nothing but ringing ears from all the time's he's hung up on me without a goodbye." Tom pouted shamelessly.

"Aw Tom, that's so sad. We'll work on Maurice. Don't you worry? Or else I'll sick Clarissa on him."

"Hmm. He does seem to be afraid of her. Okay, next there's Damien. The bodyguard, right?"

"And head of my securities team. Nobody gets near me without proper vetting by him. From my drivers who are all ex-military people to the round the clock armed security guard working surveillance at my building. By the way, Damien dealt with the whole blabby driver thing. Turns out my usual LA driver got food poisoning and needed someone to cover fast, and that guy was a mistake. I'm sorry." She still felt terrible about the whole misunderstanding.

Tom waved away her apology since all of that stuff led to him getting to know her, as far as he was concerned.

"Back to the intense security measures. I mean wow! That seems a bit extreme doesn't it?" He asked, clearly perplexed at the levels of safety she had in place.

"I've received death threats before. And my fair share of aggressive stalkers over the years. I may wander around town free as a bird, but Clarissa and Damien keep me as safe and protected as can be." she explained.

Tom's face paled as he listened to her words. Now he understood her reasons why. While he'd never felt especially threatened by his fans, maybe it was a man thing, but he did keep a bodyguard or two on staff for public events.

"Since you can never be too careful, you can add me to your list of protectors." He said sweetly, loving the sight of her cheeks turning rosy once again. "Okay, let's see who else I know by name. Terrence, your stylist?"

"Yes, he does it all. Hair, makeup, clothes. He's fantastic and also my other best friend. I have a great idea. You should bring Maurice!" December offered.

"I don't know if he'd be up for it. He doesn't seem like a celebrating kind of guy"

"You never know. He might surprise you. Anyway it's a sixty-eight year old's surprise birthday party. And there are ground rules that she insists upon."

"How is it a surprise if she already knows?" Tom asked bemused.

"Right? She insists on this party every year, which she plans and still calls it a surprise. Anyway, she likes wine coolers on her special day. So please don't judge her. Or rat her out like she thinks someone might do one day"

"I wouldn't dream of it." he said sincerely.

"Thank you. Also, she picks out all the songs to sing on karaoke and we all have to participate. So there will be shots involved for the rest of us."

"I've got an awful singing voice."

"I'm sure you're wonderful. However, it's mandatory, so you can't get out of it. She's so controlling, she even assigns the song. And not to scare you off, but there's really bad dancing involved. Like really, really bad."

"How could that be? You're a great dancer."

"Well Nunny's kind of an awful dancer, so we do our worst to make her feel at ease. Also it's pretty hilarious after three shots of tequila."

"So what you're saying to me is definitely bring a video recorder" Tom laughed.

"Please don't." December begged, hiding her smile behind her steaming drink.

"You wouldn't be in Malaysia next Friday, would you?" he asked after taking a large sip from his latte.

"Pretty sure I'm not. Why do you ask?"

"I have a movie premiering..."

"His Coy Mistress?" December cut him off excitedly, her eyes alight.

She'd been looking forward to seeing the historical drama all year. She loved all of his movies.

"Yes actually. How did you know that?" Tom gave her a strangely amused look that she didn't much care for.

"Never mind that. Get back to what you were saying." she tugged down the hat over her red tinged ears, unwilling to surrender that particular piece of information.

"Anyway, I would be honored to have you as my date for the evening." Tom said sheepishly.

"I would love to go with you but I'll be in Philly most of that week. The orphanage reconstruction starts on Thursday, but first there's a lot of paperwork and red tape to go through to make sure it all goes smoothly. I'm so sorry."

"Don't be. That's way more important. But if you do find yourself free at any point, I'll be there for the next two weeks."

"I'll keep that in mind."

"You do that."

Chapter Seventeen

Tom and December spent as much time as they could together during the weeks that followed, filling the time with long dates and phone calls before Tom's overseas trip. Like any new romance, they felt the impending separation keenly.

December even wrote a song about her feelings, the third night after he left. She even titled it 'Bereft'. But Clarissa, after hearing the first draft, quite rightly talked her out of it.

"Seriously, sweetie, it's a terrible song. Sorry I'm not sorry." she said shrugging, while stuffing her face full of marshmallows. She stretched out on the king-sized bed that the three of them shared and ignored the dirty look December threw her way.

Terrence and Clarissa had both come along to help with the children's home renovations, and to keep December's sniveling company. She missed Tom like crazy and even their daily phone call didn't help abate the space his absence left. Sharing a hotel room with two of the most cynical people in the universe didn't help much, either; they only mildly tolerated her pining. And boy, did she pine.

"I'm with C-bear. That song was all kinds of 'No Thank You'." Terrence called out from the bathroom, where he spent every free minute preening. Finding a new love interest did wonders for his broken heart. Not to mention, the birth of Damien and Marilyn's daughter, Sophie, whom they all fell in love with from the second they laid eyes on her.

"I kind of hate you both right now. Please leave." December mumbled into her pillow. She desperately wanted to sulk and they were totally harshing her vibe.

"Not going to happen, sugar pie. We cleared our schedules for you. And we're going to make you pay for that poor decision." Clarissa said as she flipped randomly through TV channels. December harrumphed through Terrence's cackles of laughter.

"Ooh Tom's on TV, Dee." Clarissa said turning up the volume on "Celebrity News" with Dana Goldwyn.

"What? Really?" She practically fell off the bed as she abruptly sat up.

Terrence rushed into the room, his newly dyed hair in disarray. The threesome cooed over how handsome he looked in his Yves St Laurent suit.

"We've been hearing rumors that you and a certain December Brown have been spending time together..." Dana asked him

Tom chuckled, a particularly goofy grin played upon his handsome features.

"Yes, she's great"

The trio held hands and squealed.

"So you like her, then?" The reporter teased

"I wouldn't exactly say like... wait, wait, that's not what I meant. That came out wrong." Tom stuttered and back tracked, his face flushing a bright red.

December made a choking, whimpering sound, her bottom lip quivering.

"Ugh he's a Publicists' nightmare, that one. No wonder they keep him out of the tabloids. He's a big dummy." Clarissa murmured, rubbing December's leg in consolation.

"He adores you. Please don't cry." Terrence cooed, crawling over to sit beside her.

"I'm not going to cry. I'm fine." she said stubbornly, even though her eyes were filled with unshed tears that she tried to will away.

"Wait, he's not done talking." Clarissa pointed out.

"Dana, can I please have a minute? I just want to clear up what I said before." Tom implored, looking flustered and desperate.

"Sure, Tom, if you think it would help." the journalist said doubtfully. She gave him a pitying look.

"I think December Brown is beautiful and fantastic. She makes me want to be a better person. I was just nervous to say it before but I have such a huge crush on her." His face was one of earnest sincerity.

"Wow. So you'd be willing to date her?" Dana stared, shocked and delighted at his impromptu confession on her show.

"If she'd have an idiot like me, I'd be the happiest man alive." Tom stared straight into the camera and right into December's heart.

"Did he just say that on TV?" December asked quietly.

"He definitely did." Clarissa answered back, just as quietly. The three of them sat in stunned silence while commercials played on the now abandoned television.

"Like on real TV?" she queried dumbly.

"Is there another kind of TV that I'm not aware of?" Terrence pondered sarcastically.

"He just did that for real, and I'm not having one of my particularly elaborate Tom daydreams?" she muttered in awe.

"Woman, we just said yes like three times." he sassed, growing tired of her slower than cold molasses reaction.

"I need to go see him." December announced, finally accepting the facts.

"Now?" Terrence and Clarissa exchanged worried looks.

"Yes. Wait. Where is he now?" She wondered if he was in Thailand now or was he in South Korea yet? She couldn't remember what Tom had told her the night before. Her brain was officially incoherent mush.

"Probably asleep." Terrence replied, dryly.

"Terrence, I swear to God…" she snapped, jerking out of her stupor to glower at him.

"Dee, calm down. I can call Maurice and organize everything. He has a premiere tomorrow night or something right? I'll take care of everything. Just breathe." Clarissa soothed, shooting Terrence a warning glance.

After Clarissa made sure they wouldn't have a slap fight, she left to make a few phone calls in the other room.

"He wants to date me." December murmured wistfully, after slipping back into a dazed state.

"You two were already dating, sweetie." Terrence remarked softly, with renewed patience.

"No. I mean, Yes. I know, but this is like official stuff, right? He's super private like me. And he just told the world. This is big."

"This is good. Actually more than that, it means he seriously digs you." Agreeing, Terrence's wide eyes matched her own, as the words sunk in.

"Okay. Everything's all set. You two are leaving first thing in the morning for Japan for the weekend. I'll stay behind to make sure all the paperwork has been filed and completed for the orphanage renovations to begin, and that the furniture orders are on schedule. So once you get back, we can officially start without any delays." Clarissa announced coming back into the room.

"Yay! I love Japan. I have to call David, to let him know." Terrence grabbed his cell phone, heading towards the terrace for privacy.

"Thank you, C. seriously." December felt guilty about ditching her plans to go chasing after Tom. But not guilty enough to not do it. At least leaving Clarissa in charge guaranteed success, so she was able to swallow down the slight hesitation that ate at her.

"Don't thank me. Thank Maurice. He's got a soft spot for Tom. Also he was the one spreading those rumors about you two. So after I called him on it, he was very eager to please. Damien is on paternity leave but don't worry about security. Maurice will handle it since you're going to be with Tom. We're keeping it as a surprise until tomorrow night, so don't say a word to him. You're already on the list as his plus one." she listed rapidly in her brusque business tone.

December hugged her tight, at a loss for words. Once again, Clarissa saved the day, and she made it seem so effortless.

"Hey now, don't you get choked up again. You know I'd do anything for you. We're sisters. Tom makes you happy, and judging from the way he handled things tonight, it's safe to say you make him happy too. Therefore I will work my magic whenever necessary, to make things easier for you two. But if he breaks your heart, I will ruin him." Clarissa declared meaningfully.

"Have I told you lately, how much I love you?" December rested her head on her best friend's shoulder.

"Not nearly as often as you should. But seriously, do we need to have a talk about contraception?" Clarissa eyes twinkled with mischief.

"Ooh I want to hear this!" Terrence intoned, coming back into room just in time. December rolled her eyes.

Terrence dabbed her eyes to give it a smoky effect as his final touch on her make up. He hummed merrily to an imaginary song while December practically vibrated with eagerness.

The long flight and subsequent lack of sleep still couldn't dampen the excitement brewing in the air.

"Voila, you are done, and you look fab." he pronounced at his own handy work.

"I always look fabulous. You're my stylist aren't you?" December said smoothly. Terrence ate it right up.

"I definitely like your attitude today." He adjusted the hem of her clingy trumpet style dress.

"You're in a good mood too. I can't believe David actually came with us. Somebody's got a boyfriend." she sing-songed as Terrence looked delighted.

"I don't know about all that, but I have to go meet up with him. He's taking me around Tokyo for the night, so don't wait up." he slipped on his leather jacket and went searching for his wallet.

"Make sure you have your room card. And have a good time" December looked on in amusement. She held up the lost item for him to see. Terrence rolled his eyes and snatched it from her.

"Yes, Mom." he said, kissing her perfumed cheek and left quickly.

December took a deep breath and exhaled shakily as a bulky bodyguard named Darius escorted her to Tom's room. She fidgeted with the strap of emerald gown as the glittering stretchy fabric clung to her curves.

"Do I look okay?" she asked nervously to the silent man walking beside her.

"You look ravishing." he answered instantly. She smiled up at him gratefully, and he returned it. She hadn't expected a 6'7" three hundred pound tattooed man to say those words to her, but it definitely did wonders to boost her confidence.

"Thanks, Darius." December said as they arrived at Tom's hotel door. She reached out and squeezed his hand for a second before knocking.

Although they'd only just met a few hours before, she liked him immediately. If he ever wanted a job stateside, she would hire him in a nanosecond.

"Good luck." he said, moving to the side to stand like a sentinel near the doorway.

"Coming." Tom called out from behind the closed door. Upon hearing his voice, December's heart began racing. She forced herself not to start hyperventilating since it would look really awkward when he opened the door.

Also Darius would probably never let her live it down.

"December!" Tom looked shocked and incredibly happy at the sight of her. "I can't believe you're actually here. You look absolutely gorgeous."

He pulled her into a tight hug, inhaling deeply. "I'm so glad you came. I really want to kiss you right now, but I don't want to ruin your makeup."

"Screw my makeup." She said, dragging his face down to hers by his tie and kissed him senseless. Even if her lipstick wasn't smudge proof, she would have done it anyway. Seeing him in his sleek black suit with his hair coiffed just right, she instantly overcame her sudden case of anxiousness.

"Excuse me. But maybe you should take this into the room." Darius interjected.

Tom looked a little dazed when December gently pushed him backwards into his hotel room, and shut the door. He cradled her face in his hands and kissed over and over again. "It hasn't even been a week yet, and I've missed you like mad."

"Me too." December replied between smooches. "I saw last night's interview and I had to come see you."

"I'm sorry about that. I really put my foot in my mouth at the start. I had to try to fix things." Tom explained, leading her over to a small angular couch. He took her hand when they were both seated, and kissed both of her palms.

"You don't have anything to apologize about. I'm happy you told the world, actually."

"Thank God, because that would have been supremely distressing if you wanted to break up." he gave her a heart-melting lopsided grin.

"So I heard you still have a crush on me?" December purred, sliding closer to him.

"Like you wouldn't believe." Tom said brushing his lips against hers.

BONUS PREVIEW

Diary of a Big Dummy

or

*Joss's Cautionary Tale of Heartbreak,
Revenge, and Possibly Murder*

by

Tamara Philip

Chapter One

Dear Diary,

Or whoever is reading this in the case of my untimely demise,

Are you as surprised as I am that I'm writing in a private journal? I'm not really the type to actually take the time and write things down. I mean, I barely do my homework.

Anyway, I've decided to put pen to paper and here we are. "Why?" you might ask, if you weren't basically a modernized papyrus scroll? Well, because my mother's best friend, Althea, called me vapid when she thought I wasn't around to overhear her.

Okay, that's a total lie since that happened like two years ago and I didn't even cry over it or anything. In all honesty, she was right but who wants to hear someone saying that behind your back? But her calling me a "vapid little twit" is still connected, in a way, to the reason I decided to write this diary.

The truth is I'm writing to you because of a boy. I know, I know, how cliché! But this wasn't just any guy. This was Jack Buckley, who practically stalked me for weeks trying to befriend me and gain my trust all while being a total hottie. The guy who made me feel entirely way too much. Jack, who I kind of, sort of, still miss even though he's a giant jerkface. Don't judge me, okay? You're a diary; you're supposed to accept me as I am. By the way, if you're an FBI agent reading this in order to solve my case, then try to be professional, will you? Sheesh.

I should just call this *"Joss' Cautionary Tale of Heartbreak, Revenge and Possibly Murder"*...minus the actual murder and revenge part. I just don't have the constitution for vengeance seeking, and I'm really bad at following through with plans.

Oh God, I'm already rambling off topic. Okay so I'll start from the beginning; from the day Jack Buckley stumbled in, and then promptly ruined my life. I just want to paint a better picture as to why the ability to get my heartbroken was such a surprise to me.

Diary of a Big Dummy

You know how there are some people who seem to sort of float through life? Fitting in and not fitting in all at once? People who are permanently behind and out of sync, but not noticeable enough to be labeled a misfit? The ones described as quirky but they really mean 'weirdo'? Yeah, that was pretty much me in a nutshell.

Okay, wait, maybe I'm not explaining it very well. For instance, my three best friends had hobbies, or at least something to be passionate about. There was Tiffany and her addiction to cute boys and leopard print anything, Maggie with her obsession with being in other people's business and telling them how to live their lives, and ever-growing collection of owl figurines, and Natalie, with her softball team and Frisbee fanaticism.

Meanwhile, I was kind of like "Yeah, okay! Calm down it's not that exciting." I meant that about life in general. I always felt like a somewhat cynical outsider looking in. Everything felt slightly worn out and faded even when it was new to me. And that was why Althea, with her snobby ways and trying-too-hard-spiked-bob called me the V-word. I only truly cared about tacos, and I was actually proud of that.

That didn't mean I was a super cool Goth or hipster. Nope, instead I was just an overall terrible person. Not like 'I've punched babies' kind of terrible. Just like 'I'm literally just skating by on the kindness of strangers because I just can't get the hang of normal things,' kind of terrible. I was horrible at sports, I hated collectibles, and I didn't find people fascinating enough to be a busybody. I wasn't even a klutz or clumsy or anything. I couldn't even get the knack of being part of society.

I mean even at 15 and a half, I still get nervous when dealing with cashiers. I literally forget how to do math and my palms get sweaty and I end up acting like a robot with faulty circuits. Like seriously, what is that? Or, when I was a kid learning to tie my shoelaces, I was so bad at it my parents just gave up and got me slip-ons or Velcro sneakers. No kidding. To this day I'm not a hundred percent sure on how to do it. Or, how my friends are all actively trying to date and I'm just not. Not interested, not sought after, not attractive. Well, not at that point, but we'll get back to that later.

Anyway, another side effect of being one of those special brand of people, besides being below average in the game of life, I also had the worst luck at everything. I mean if I even studied hard for a test, it was usually for the wrong subject. My luck was that bad!

The only thing I could ever bet on was getting things wrong or losing things. Ugh! The losing things part was the absolute worst. Which was how this whole Jack Buckley thing started...all because of me losing something.

Chapter Two

It was a craptacular day in November and I was stomping to school a half an hour late, while contemplating what I must have done to cause the universe to hate me so very much.

I'd just realized that I lost my new purple shoes sometime over the weekend, and I didn't just misplace them. Oh no, I lost them in a big way. Like, I literally might have left them in the middle of Times Square, and my brain cells wouldn't cooperate, so I couldn't remember exactly where and when I lost them. It was driving me crazy. Bleh. Those shoes were going to change my life too! They were satin and perfect and once I started wearing them I was going to finally get my life together. I'm talking studying, being fashionable, actually exfoliating. The works! Ugh, it still hurts just to think about my long lost shoes.

Why did I have to go and lose stuff again?

Diary of a Big Dummy

I was trying to figure out the answer to that particularly soul draining question when I walked right into a person with such force that it nearly threw me back onto the pavement.

I braced myself for the fall, preparing myself for the pain of a scraped palm or sore butt, except that this time it didn't happen. Instead, the jerk caught me. I opened my eyes and was about to thank my "hero" with a scathing remark when I looked up at him, but stopped in stunned amazement. Wow! What a face. A little too model perfect if you asked me but I mean even his jawline was hot. Anyway, he was probably an escaped convict, since he was staring at me with a little too much longing in his bright green eyes.

I slid my hand into my coat pocket and gripped my cellphone, just in case I needed to dial 911 in a hurry.

"Are you ok?" he asked me in a husky voice. I'm not kidding, there was definite husk in there.

"Yes, thanks for catching me. But you should really watch where you're walking." I said rather nicely as I gently pried his crazy mitts off of me. He laughed as if I said something charming.

"Uh sure thing. Do you live around here?" He asked, scratching the back of his neck. God, he was tall. Not creepy basketball player tall, but you know, hot guy tall, if that made any sense, which it probably didn't.

Especially since he was more than likely mentally unstable, I felt like a creep checking him out and I wanted to get away without provoking a possible murderous rage.

I replied slowly, so he could understand me.

"Um, no. This is a school. People do not live here. People live in houses." I gestured to the sprawling landscape that was Flushing High School. I guess it amused him since he started to laugh again, this time though it was somewhat maniacally.

Seriously, there was something wrong with that guy and I thought it best that I removed myself from the situation as quickly as possible.

A few hours later, I was staring at the very same bozo again. Except this time we were in our gym uniforms. Red bottoms and grey t-shirts. His were shorts while I wore the sweatpants option to hide my crummy legs. Unsurprisingly, he looked pretty good in his. Where was the justice in that?

I was cursing the fact that they let just about anybody into our school, when he began waving to get my attention. I quickly looked away and sighed, this was going to be a long class.

As I turned away I saw him lean over the only desk in the gymnasium. The one the teachers use to take attendance or whatever. He started filling out a blue emergency information card. I figured that he must've been new since most of us filled out those cards at the beginning of the school year. No wonder he looked so "special"; he was just lonely and awkward on his first day of school...except he seemed to know a lot of people in this class. Weird. I shrugged and kept on walking.

As usual, everyone milled around the gym until the whistle officially blew, finding either their assigned floor spots or their friends. Since I wasn't in the business of looking eager for gym, I headed over to where I knew I would find my friends in various poses of leisure on the bleachers.

"Hello, ladies who didn't wait for their bestest best friend, who was running only a little bit late this morning." I said passive aggressively. I lightly tugged Tiffany's jet black ponytail for good measure, and dodged as she tried to swat me away.

"A little late, Joss? How about 45 minutes late?" pointed out a certain redheaded minx named Natalie Flowers.

"That's subjective." I answered back, dramatically rolling my eyes. I sat down next to Maggie, who was sprawled on the bleacher beside her, busily texting away.

"Um, no, it's a fact, dummy! Time is an actual fact." she scoffed.

Damn her and her knowledge! This was why she was in all Honors classes and I was so definitely not.

"Traitorous tramps." I grumbled. The girls laughed and threw paper balls at me.

"Ew, did you find those in the bleachers?!" I shrieked. That only made them cackle louder.

Maggie Aboud, Tiffany Chung, and I, along with Natalie, have been best friends since we were a bunch of plucky 9 year olds who got in trouble for tripping boys for fun. In our defense, they asked for it by running through a joint hopscotch-jump rope girls-only area. Up until that point, we were virtually strangers, even though we'd all been in the same school since kindergarten. We had each individually thought it was a good idea to teach those jerks a lesson, but nobody believed us when we said that. Naturally, getting punished for being wise-guys brought the four of us closer, and we've been inseparable ever since. Skip forward nearly 8 years later, and here we are in high school with our friendship stronger than ever.

We were joking around when a dark cloud, also known in French as 'le stalker,' came upon us. Ugh, could he go away already? Stupid Captain Linger. We only just bumped into each other and now he was making me regret not using pepper spray on him. I know what you're thinking. If he's so good looking, why are you mad that he's trying to be friendly? I'll tell you why. I just don't trust guys that are insanely cute. They were probably shifty and conniving and stuff. I know this for a fact because I've seen tons of movies on the Lifetime channel and they're pretty much like documentaries....no matter what Natalie says.

"Hi girls, can I talk your friend for a second?" he asking grinning with blindingly perfect white teeth. He probably had braces for years. He just couldn't have been that lucky in the gene department.

"Yes! Take her! Whatever!" we all said. Wait a minute, it was only me responding, and damn it, it was me he was expecting to talk to.

"Oops, haha, I guess I could spare a minute." I slid sheepishly out of my seat and tried to ignore the curious stares of my nosey friends.

"What's up?" I asked as I sauntered over to him.

I took the opportunity to quickly check him out. He really was very easy on the ol' eyeholes, I guess. If you were into golden haired Calvin Klein models, that is. I wasn't, so I was lost to why he was seeking me out, of all people? Yeah sure, I was awesome and a general delight to know but until today I'd never laid eyes on the guy. However, it wasn't too much of a stretch to say I was not going to be his type.

I was easily described as a short, roundish thing. At 5 feet tall with dark brown curly hair to go with dark brown eyes and medium brown complexion, I was pretty enough that I took great school photos but I wasn't going to be storming any fashion runways. I even wore glasses. I had little to no real fashion sense, or common sense, actually come to think of it. I was nothing like the pretty boy standing before me, with his good posture and his trendy haircut. Okay, so maybe I was being a little judgmental. Big whoop.

Honestly, I wasn't expecting anything amazing out of this conversation. He probably wanted to borrow lunch money or something. I eyed him warily, waiting for his reply.

"I don't think we were ever properly introduced. I'm Jack, and I know you're Joss. You know, we've been in the same school for almost 3 years and this the first time we've ever interacted." he said, sticking his hand out so we could shake. I stared at it, puzzled, but awkwardly took his outstretched hand in mine. What teenaged boy shakes hands with a strange girl?

"Uh, okay. Wait a minute, so does that you mean you aren't new?" I was confused as to how he knew my name and why didn't I know there was actual gorgeous dudes in this school? I mean, where was I all this time?

Jack chuckled dryly. "You would think that, wouldn't you? Actually, we have two classes together this semester. And I sit behind you in one of them. Does that ring any bells?" It didn't but he seemed genuinely interested in my response.

"Um sure, I guess... anyway can you tell me what this is about? I was having a very important discussion with my classmates before you interrupted." I asked impatiently, my eyes wandered around the gym in lieu of making the eye contact that I saw he was trying to initiate.

I totally wasn't, but whatever. I was clearly looking for a hasty exit out but he wouldn't take the hint. Luckily, the whistle blew and saved me from an increasingly boring conversation. I mean obviously, I didn't know who he was, nor did I care to.

I hustled away quickly as he yelled at my retreating back "We'll talk more later!"

What for? He didn't say anything mind-blowing in the first place.

I re-joined my friends on the gym floor in our class assigned order, while we waited for our teacher.

"So what did Jack Buckley want?" Tiffany whispered, sitting cross-legged to my right.

"Holy crap! You know who he is? How come you never told me?" I whispered back, surprised.

"That's because you're totally oblivious. Everybody knows Jack." she said rolling her eyes. I scowled at her.

Maggie turned halfway around from her spot in front of Tiffany. "Tell us already, what'd he want with you?"

"Boring stuff. He called me over and then just wasted my time. He just wanted to borrow my textbook."

"That was it? That's lame." Tiffany and Maggie shot each other a look which I chose to ignore. Thankfully, Coach Schwartz finally waltzed in carrying the dreaded volleyball. God, I hated playing volleyball. Who wants to be hit in the face for like 45 minutes? Not me, that's for sure.

I was relieved that my lie seemed to satisfy them. I don't know why I didn't just tell them what Jack said but I figured since he didn't really say anything important, then there was no need for them to be getting excited over nothing. They went absolutely bananas over anything to do with boys, so that wouldn't take much. It would only lead to way too many phone calls about a guy who was clearly simple in the brains.

Chapter Three

I loved three o' clock. During the week, it meant that school was over and we were free to roam the streets on the way home. Even when it was freezing cold out, we still had fun giggling and munching on cheap snacks from the little bodega near the school. On this particular day though, Maggie and Tiffany were both singing along loudly to some song that we were pretty sure they got the words all sorts of wrong to before we started talking about boys. Specifically, how confusing they were.

"I don't know what you're all so surprised about. Guys do that kind of thing, like, all the time! It's even written in the history books. Boys are insane!" Maggie wailed.

163

"But why do they have to be insane? Why can't they just be normal? Why can't they just stop confusing me? I mean...us!" Tiffany whined.

Natalie and I silently stuffed our mouths full of potato chips since this could go on all afternoon. We might as well enjoy the show. Maggie was always the wise expert on the male species and Tiffany was always the worst. She was the emotional one of the group.

Tiffany was upset because this boy called George Bustamante, who she was secretly in love with for the past 3 months, had suddenly stopped talking to her.

Although they weren't going out or anything, since she never told him how she felt, there was definitely some potential there. They flirted like crazy from third period until the final bell of the school day. Chatting away happily and touching each other in that shy lovely way people who like each other do, but now? Nothing. He just ceased to acknowledge her existence anymore. He didn't sit next to her in Chemistry like he usually did. George just froze her out overnight, so understandably, she was enraged.

"What am I supposed to do now that he's not speaking to me anymore? What should I do? Should I text him and find out what's wrong?" Tiffany asked, looking slightly twitchy.

"Don't do anything. Just pretend like he doesn't exist either. Do not even think about texting him or else you'll look desperate." Maggie urged.

"She's right, Tiff. Listen to her, she's the sane one of us, remember? That alone should earn your trust." I said as I peered into an empty bag of salt and vinegar chips, searching for any hidden pieces.

"Maybe he was sick today and he didn't want you to get sick too, so that's why he kept his distance." said sweet, naive Natalie, which caused us to stare at her as if she'd grown an extra eye.

"Well, it could happen." she added under her breath.

"Anyway, now you have to swear, Tiffany. Swear that you won't text or call him for 24 hours. Okay?" Maggie demanded, holding up her pinkie.

"I swear..." She answered reluctantly and intertwined her finger with Maggie's. She was totally going to call him and we all knew it. Even in kindergarten you knew a pinkie swear from Tiffany Chung was not a binding agreement. Maggie shot her only the slightest of skeptical looks before turning on me.

"Now you, Missy! Tell us about Jack and his supposed textbook borrowing."

I nearly choked on Natalie's Raisinets that I was scarfing down like there was no tomorrow. She glared at me with her shrewd gray eyes, and I started stuttering. If she doesn't become an interrogator for law enforcement, it'll be a damn shame. Maggie Aboud always seemed to know when a person was trying to hide something from her and she always got the truth out of you by the time she was done with you.

"Who? Oh, him. Hmm, well nothing to tell, just a textbook. Good grief, don't act as if it's never happened before." I answered back, hotly. I really hated when someone doubted my lies. Seriously, where was the trust?

"You're trying to tell me that one of the hottest guys in our school, Jack Buckley, went out of his way to ask you to borrow your textbook?" Maggie asked, incredulously.

"Um, yeah, hello? It's not that unheard of to borrow books from classmates." I tried not to sound defensive but the guilt was killing me. She quirked her eyebrows, amused, as if she could see my rusty brain cells working overtime.

"He asked you, of all people? Okay, I'll buy it. So, what class was it for?" she asked in that Maggie way. Like she knew you were lying but wanted to see how far you were willing to carry on. In my case, I was willing to go the distance.

"Um, Science." I said, taking a chance. None of them had that particular class with me, and hopefully they didn't know his schedule either. They looked at one another knowingly and then back at me, so I hurriedly changed the subject.

"So, I heard it's going to be a huge snowfall tonight and classes might be closed. You do know we're having a snowball fight, right?" That got them all talking, much to my relief.

The next morning, I woke up and squealed with delight when I saw that the snow storm had done its job. I was excited for any day off from school but snow days were my absolute favorite. I called up the girls to make plans to meet up after breakfast then I woke up my kid sister to see if she wanted to come along, but she wasn't too crazy about snow. After she told me off about waking her up for dumb reasons, she ended up making me late. Maggie called to say they'd meet me there, so I quickly bundled up to face the cold.

Trudging to the park, my thoughts were filled with all of the awesome things we'd do until it got too cold to stay out any longer. Therefore, I didn't even realize that the cute weirdo from school was walking towards me until he stopped directly in my way.

Jack smiled brightly down at me. "Hi, Joss."

I sighed loudly.

Who cares if he looked really hot in his bright blue ski hat which brought out his eyes? He was probably just showing off.

"Oh, it's you." I looked further up the road past him in case I saw anyone I actually knew and cared to see.

"Are you heading to the park? I heard there was going to be sled races and everything." He said, annoyingly, like I cared.

"Yeah, I guess."

"Cool, me too. Let's walk together, then." he said. I shrugged and pulled my fluffy hot pink earmuffs further down over my rapidly freezing ears and led the way.

"That color looks nice on you."

I didn't know whether he was being serious or making fun of me, but when I looked up at him with narrowed eyes, he looked nothing but sincere.

"Oh, thanks. I like your hat." I said lamely. I mean his hat was okay, I guess, but it was his face that deserved the compliments.

"Are you a model?" I blurted out. I couldn't help myself, I needed to know.

"Um…"

"Oh my God! You *are* a model! Why are you in Flushing High School? Don't you have more glamorous places to be?"

"Fine, I'll admit it. I did the older boys collection for Marshalls and Sears last year. But, it was only to make extra money to buy my Xbox and stuff."

"Uh huh. You'll probably do it again in college or whatever. In between acting gigs or working at Starbucks." Jack shot me an amused glance.

"You're the only one at school who knows. Can you just keep it a secret for now? Please?"

"Duh, of course I won't tell. Hey, Jack, can I ask you a question?"

"Sure, you can ask me anything." He was all charm and pearly whites. Trouble with a capital 'T'.

"Well, I was just wondering…why are you being so friendly to me all of a sudden? I mean, it's like you said, we've been in the same school for years and we never spoke before so what's the big deal now?" I asked, squinting up at him.

"I don't know. Things seem different now… like our paths have finally crossed and I didn't want to miss my chance." he replied, quickly glancing my way.

"Miss your chance?" I asked, with a frown.

"Yes, to be friends. Wouldn't that be great?" He asked cheerfully. Ew, who says stuff like that?

"...Friends. Okay then, I guess. I just want you to know that I think you're very brave to be going to a normal school when you're, you know, not normal." Jack started laughing loudly as we entered the park.

"Well, I gotta go, bye!" And I ran off to where I saw Natalie and the others waving me over.

This was by far one of the best snow days that we've had. Everyone froze their butts off, but we were having lots of fun with snowball fights and sledding on any little hill we could find. We were even going to go to Maggie's house after, for hot chocolate. But, of course my luck couldn't hold because as I was bending down to roll a big ball of snow to be the first part of my snowman, the zipper on my jeans broke and it refused to close or even go back up.

"Ugh... not again" I mumbled to myself. I was wearing thermal leggings so my jeans were fitting a little snug. Now that the zipper split wide open, you could see my pink heart thermals bulging out in the worst way possible. And it was just my luck that my sweater and winter coat fell just above the zipper line. I was struggling to hide my exposed undergarments when someone tapped me on the shoulder. I turned around and there was Jack, all red-nosed but happy.

"Hey, you! Wanna race?" He chirped.

Oh for goodness sake. Now I think of myself as a charitable person, but this was getting to be too much.

"Um, I'm a little busy." I growled as I tried in vain to keep my bulge covered.

"Come on, just one little race with your new best friend." he whined.

"Oh, geez! Fine. Let's just do this." I bellowed and grabbed my sleigh and walked over to the snow covered hill with stupid Jack trailing behind.

"Ready? I'll go first." I said throwing down my sled and prepared myself for the ride. I stumbled and fell onto my back into the wooden sleigh just as I started down the hill, so I didn't look as graceful as I had hoped. And when I looked down, all I could see was my unzipped pants so naturally, I started to panic. I was like a turtle on its back, struggling to flip over yet I kept on fussing around with my short coat, trying in vain to make it stretch. Jack's sled came speeding towards mine while I was still exposed and mortified.

"Hey, what's wrong with your zipper?" my mortal enemy, Jack, called out as he looked straight at my patterned bulge as we slid down the hill.

Why me?

Book Club Discussion Guide

The Trouble with Playing Cupid
by Tamara Philip

(1) Have you ever played matchmaker? Did the to-be-matched people know it was happening?

(2) How would you react to being matched in a surprise move on a live TV show?

(3) What character(s) did you identify with most?

(4) Do Tom and December remind you of anyone you know?

(5) If you had to describe this book in just one word, what would it be?

(6) How would you have handled the media frenzy?

(7) What made you realize Tom and December would have their own HEA?

Tamara Philip

After spending most of her life in New York City, Tamara Philip decided to let love lead her on an international adventure, where she's met many amazing people and ate entirely too much. Tamara and her English-born fiance, Chris, now split their time between the United Kingdom and The Caribbean.

The Trouble with Playing Cupid is her debut novel, and writing has been her secret passion since childhood. Quirky female leads are her trademark.

On any given day you can find Tamara telling people what to do, dodging wedding planning, and working hard on her second novel.

Where to find Tamara Philip online

Website: TamaraPhilipWrites.wordpress.com
Twitter: @MsTamaraPhilip
Facebook: https://www.facebook.com/TamaraPhilipwrites